Now It Begins

A Novella

Cliff Mulvihill

Yellow Finch Publications

Yellow Finch books may be purchased for study groups or
other educational use. For information please write: Yellow
Finch Publications, 2029 N Melborn, Dearborn, Michigan,
48128. Or e-mail at yellow.finch@sbcglobal.net

ISBN: 0-9785790-0-3
ISBN-13: 978-0-9785790-0-5

Manufactured in the United States

Introduction

The motivation for this novella came with my aware-
ness that there was an absence of information about
the Christ as a youngster and as a young man. When so
much has been written about Him regarding his birth and
then again about his ministry and death, why was there an
absence of information regarding the interim years?

The answer for me was simple. He was absent. But how
do we account for the absence?

Now It Begins is a tale of a spiritual journey told to the
disciples by a young scholar who had a close association
with the Christ as a man. The young scholar, now called
Phillip, relates all that he knows. The disciples he speaks to
are in hiding. They await their own demise or instructions
from their leaders, also in hiding. The group Phillip speaks
with is headed by Mark.

Mark and Phillip engage in a lengthy conversation as

Phillip recites his tale. The tale involves several journeys over many years. You will please note that when Mark is speaking his words appear in italics. When Phillip is speaking his words appear in regular type. I hope the use of this convention will heighten your enjoyment of this story.

Cliff Mulvihill
Dearborn
May 8, 2006

Now It Begins

He came to us while we were still in hiding. We always kept the wicks of the oil lamp low and our conversation quiet. The women brought him to us. They could come and go. Why do women need to hide?

Those were troubled times. The crucifixion put a scare into everyone. We fled to safe places and secret dwellings. We did not go out. The women tended to the gravesite because they could come and go without much notice. For the men there were Roman guards and temple guards and betrayers everywhere. It was not safe.

For me, I was staying in the house of a friend. He was sympathetic to our beliefs and housed a few of us in a room above the street. The room was comfortable enough though it grew hot during the day. We had woven fiber mats to sleep on and one window for light. By night we could sit on the roof to keep cool. By day we had to endure the heat lest we give away our host. He was not wealthy as you might think, but he was comfortable enough to keep us in food and drink until our leaders could determine what we should do. He never asked for payment. We learned later that some of our number were required to pay for their lodgings. I was fortunate.

Our leaders were out of the city. In time they would return. But for now they were living with friends and sympathizers as could be found. Some who were friends before the crucifixion were not friends afterward, as you might guess. They were afraid too.

We communicated of course. Usually communication took several days. We would not come and go in the same day you see. Under disguise or cover of darkness we would venture forth to one house or another for the purpose of prayer and discussion. There was much more discussion than prayer I can assure you. Then we would return in a day or two to pass on what we had learned.

Peter was as scared as any of us and provided no leadership in those early days. James was certain that the movement would continue but was indecisive as to what should be done. Then Son of Sander came to us. He was now known as Phillip. Why the women guided him to us rather than to some other members outside of the city in better locations I do not know. He was not counted among us and had nothing to fear from the authorities yet he stayed with us in hiding for many days. Here is what he told us.

The dust clouds that did not settle on animal or human hung in the air and drifted imperceptibly back to earth.

Kicked up by each footfall the dust clung to clothing, faces, carts, became one with the food, and mixed with the breathable air giving the air texture and a choking dry taste. Those on horseback rode above the dust. Those outriders had a job to do. They were to watch for bandits or otherwise assist in keeping the caravan moving. Levi out front, always Levi out front.

Yeshua, in the rearmost position with the sheep and goats, plodded on. I don't think he could see or hear Levi the dust obscuring vision and dampening sound. His walk had long since become hypnotic. The sheep and goats accustomed to following along. Little need to be mindful of them. His walking meditations reminding him that his ancient ancestors had been called the "dusty ones." The dusty ones were not always welcomed in the places they passed through. But they were following Yahweh to who knew where. The next watering place? The next revelation? It must have been like this for them. Walking in the dust. Keeping a lookout for hostile people who might be lying in wait to plunder the caravan and run the sheep and goats off. Always the dust. Yeshua wondered if Levi resembled in any way the leadership and strength that Abraham showed his people, the dusty ones.

This trek had been profitable. The way home lay ahead to the south and a bit to the west with hopefully more profit. We were still traveling north. With good weather and Yahweh's blessing (Levi would say good fortune) we would all make it safely home. But that was for the future to tell. There were many byways that had to be traveled on this pilgrimage before one could think of home.

Levi was the son of a caravan master who had followed in his father's footsteps. Yeshua never believed that Levi was his real name. He had a vague memory of Levi being called by another name during that first trip to Egypt. But he was very young on that first trip. This was Yeshua's third trip with Levi. That's where I met Yeshua. I was just a boy then, not very old really. . . . But I'm sorry, friends, I am getting ahead of myself.

I am now called Phillip. My new masters gave me that name. When I first met Yeshua I was called Son of Sander. I will relate all that I know. That which Yeshua told me along the way and that which I have come to know while residing in his mother's house these past weeks. Recent events I have just learned. But of course, you already know.

The Journey With No Children

Let me tell you what I know by asking you a question. How do you begin a spiritual journey, gentlemen? Mark, when did your begin yours? I tell you now that you probably do not know. Yeshua did not realize until much later when his journey actually began. I think we can see the beginnings of it during those early days. I will tell you of his first journey. The one with no children.

That first trip had not been as exciting and adventurous as the second. Yeshua told me his parents were anxious and maybe even afraid. He was too young to remember all of the details. He wasn't even sure why the sudden need for a trip, but sudden it was. One day he was playing in a tree outside the house, the next day his mother was gathering their belongings and packing them into a cart.

"But mother why must we go? Whose cart is that?" Yeshua was always asking questions. The cart appeared used and dirty to young Yeshua. But it was sturdy enough. It would carry their few belongings.

"Your father said we must leave. He bought the cart for us. You will ride on top."

You might imagine, sitting on top of their belongings and riding along in the cart would seem like a grand and wonderful thing for a child. Being on top of the cart gave him an advantage in seeing far off. He could see Levi's father out in front. The biggest and strongest man he had ever seen. His own father was strong and could lift large stones and great beams of wood. But he was not strong like Levi's father.

His mother and father had to walk. Yeshua could see many people walking. There were also other carts, camels, donkeys, and horses. Only strong men rode the horses. The camels had bundles tied to their sides. Men walking beside the camels carrying sticks. He was the only child riding in a cart. He was the only child making the trip.

His father walking quickly ahead, approaching a man on horseback, "Why are we moving so slow?" Looking back at his mother, "Surely we must travel faster than this."

"Traveling in large groups is slow. What's your hurry? We get there when we get there. We travel together for safety. If we travel too fast, we leave stragglers. Stragglers are bad luck."

Rejoining them, his father took his mother aside to speak quietly to her in harsh loud whispers. They had been doing that more and more lately. When he was within hearing they would talk quietly or not at all. This was something new. Yeshua was not used to being left out of family conversation and had a little boy's concern for not being included, a feeling of being left out.

Spying a stick, Yeshua jumped down from the cart, grabbed up the stick, and clambered back aboard. He pretended he was a great warrior riding in a fine chariot, though he told me he didn't know what a warrior was back then. Neither had he seen a chariot except at a great distance. The donkey pulling the cart was his armored-clad warhorse. The sun beat down on the mighty warrior and, as the day progressed, reduced him to a thirsty, tired little boy in need of sleep. He settled under the leather covering and into the belongings and tried to get comfortable. But no comfort was to be had. With their belongings mixed in with father's tools, no soft place could be found. Still, in time, he dozed.

"Yeshua, hide among the belongings!" The shout from his father awakened him, but he didn't know what he was supposed to do. He was confused.

"I said hide," his father yelled between his teeth as he shoved Yeshua's head and then the rest of him down into the cart.

"Hurry, there are riders coming!" urged his mother as she clasped her hands to her breast.

Hearing his mother's distress made him scramble down amongst the family belongings even further. He couldn't see out and didn't think anyone could see in. He told me that he was more afraid of his father's anger at that moment than anything else. Never had his father treated him so roughly.

Never had he seen his mother so worried. He said that he did as he was told not wanting to anger his father further. Squirming from the cramped position he was in he began to perspire. He tried to hold his breath and not move. He didn't know where the danger was. But his parents thought he was in danger. So he hid. The caravan stopped moving.

It was now clear that the riders were soldiers, three of them. Yeshua could not see them but he could hear his mother and father talking. They were standing near the donkey. Now father began yelling at mother, "What a worthless donkey we have purchased!"

He could hear the sounds of horses riding by, but not too close. Yeshua could not understand why his parents were afraid. He was sure it had nothing to do with the donkey.

The soldiers rode by, not giving anyone or anything a second glance. They stopped at the front of the caravan to speak with Levi's father. He took his time looking back over the entire length of his caravan: the camels and the camel drivers, the donkey carts, and finally his own horsemen. He turned to face his questioners with purpose. He shook his head slowly, but with authority.

The horsemen rode off.

Were they soldiers trying to make some quick money for themselves by enforcing a tax or exacting money from the caravan? Were they sent by the king in search of small children? We will never know. Remember, friends? It was rumored and later confirmed by others that male children were taken. There was great mourning. Many families in other places suffered the loss of their male children. For the moment anyway, Yeshua had been spared

Yeshua told me that he remembered his father showing some relief at the departure of the soldiers. But for days afterwards he was on constant watch for anything out of the ordinary. Yeshua had to stay near the cart by orders from his father.

By and by Yosuf and Miriam and Yeshua found refuge in the land of Egypt.

Yes, Phillip, we remember the scriptures. Egypt was a land of refuge for out ancestors in times of famine. Apparently it proved to be a land of refuge again?

I believe you are correct, Mark. Yeshua's father and mother were able to hide him away for some time. They kept him separate from any danger. It was here his awakening began to stir, I think.

Let me continue the story for you, as I understand it. Yeshua didn't know about Egypt then. He had only heard it mentioned and passed it off as adult talk. Their trek was slow. The ride atop the cart was not as glorious as that first day. But as the days went on Yeshua's parents were more and more tolerant of his walking beside the donkey or along side one of the camel drivers. In the days immediately after the incident with the horsemen, Yeshua made sure he did everything he was told and responded immediately to his parents' wishes. But after several days of travel, with their home further and further behind, he began to venture off the cart and mix with the others. There was not much for him to do. He was the only child on the trip. He could ride in the cart or walk.

The rising sun was no longer off his left shoulder. The setting sun met him full in the face each afternoon making the afternoons all the more intolerable. He had the sense that the caravan had turned somehow to head due west, but couldn't remember when such a turn had occurred. This mystery unfolded at the watering hole.

The caravan master's son was in charge of the herds of sheep and goats. Even at that young age Yeshua knew that this was not a very high station, but the son seemed proud to do what his father had asked. The sheep and goats were not in so great a number that they could be called herds, but that is what he said they were. After the beasts of burden had been watered, the sheep and goats were watered. This seemed to be the order of things: First the men (and their horses if they rode), then the women and camels and donkeys, and then the sheep and goats. Yeshua had gotten used to this and would run ahead at each oasis, having become emboldened to leaving his parents' side.

Here the shepherd would talk about the caravan, who was nice and who was mean, the direction of travel and the mystery of the sun rising in the east and setting in the west each day. The shepherd was not a child he could play with, neither was he a man fully grown. All Yeshua knew was that the shepherd was older and smarter than he was. His parents would talk with him, but mostly the other grown ups paid him little attention, unless he was underfoot or asked too many questions. The shepherd, though, would talk and laugh and tell Yeshua stories about how one day he would be a great caravan master like his father.

"Some day I will lead a great caravan. We will go north and trade and bring goods and we will always make a profit. The bandits will not even think to raid us because we will be too strong. The merchants will love us because we deal honorably."

"Which way is north?"

The shepherd pointed.

"How do you know?"

"Face the rising sun."

Yeshua faced east.

"When you face the rising sun, north is always on your left." And just to prove to his young pupil that he was indeed knowledgeable about directions said, "At night you can tell which way is north by finding a certain star. I will show it to you some night. It will be good for you to learn your way in the world."

The food was never plentiful, but Yeshua never went hungry. His mother saw to that. At times they would buy food along the way. Some dried meat or dried fruit. Once they had fish. Usually the women would make their own bread early in the morning before the sun came up. Bread and a hot drink for breakfast. The caravan did not stop for a mid day meal. You had to eat while you walked, if you ate at all. Often Yeshua would hoist himself up on the cart and eat a piece of goat cheese, trying to keep the dust off it as he ate. He didn't like eating dust. The evening meal was the exciting time. Sometimes local people would come to the caravan to sell things, mostly food. It was at the evening meal that his parents kept him close, still distrustful of strangers.

Once mother urged father to buy a goat so they could slaughter it and eat fresh meat. Father said no. We didn't have enough money, the trip was lasting longer than he expected. Soon we would arrive. Soon, all would be well.

What little he could understand about Egypt with its wonders and great cities led Yeshua to believe the little village they came to settle in was not Egypt. There were no wonders only small hut-like dwellings in which men and women lived. From what I could gather, it was a very poor place. Yeshua didn't dwell on the particulars of this village. You must remember that he was yet a small boy. Some of the men worked from their huts. But they shooed him away. Too many questions. A boy under foot. Some of the men went off to find work.

His father was one of those. He would be gone sometimes for days at a time but mostly just overnight. He would come back with food and a few coins and be gone again by morning. Yeshua didn't have much of a memory of this man, this father, who came and went in his early years.

His early memory was of his mother who cared for him, loved him, but mostly watched out that no harm came to him. She told him stories about Abraham and Noah. She played with him. They made a game of fetching water. Her laughter brought a smile to his face until he was laughing too. Although he didn't really know why he was laughing except that his mother was laughing and he couldn't help himself.

When his sister was born, Yeshua found that mother

was very busy. Yeshua could wander away for a time without his mother knowing where he was. He could not sit at home all day. He wanted to be out. When she would fret over little sister Yeshua would slip out for a time and amuse himself at the well or under a tree. Though he did watch the baby sometimes when his mother went to fetch water or to talk with the other women.

The real adventures came when his brother was born. The stories were still good; his mother's presence was a comfort to him, especially when father was gone. But with a newborn and a one-year old to care for there was less time for him. So he began wandering further and further from home.

Yeshua passed on many of his early discoveries to me. You must remember that I was just a boy myself when he shared these things with me. He discovered a small grove of trees that was good for tree climbing or sitting in the shade. He discovered that flies bite and could leave large welts on your skin. Snakes didn't move very fast in the early morning but could really scramble over the ground after they warmed up. It was good to walk with a stick in your hand. You shouldn't get very far from home when you were hungry. Running felt good especially into the wind. (We actually ran together when a strong wind was blowing. He always let me win.) It was fun to jump off large rocks or splash in puddles after a rain. But his best discovery was an old man.

Wandering away south on the opposite side of this little village he came upon an old man sitting by a large boulder. He was a slightly plump old man with an unkempt beard and a dark robe that was musty with small tears in it here and there. The man seemed to be singing but there was no one there to sing to. A curious thing.

"Hello," Yeshua said tentatively.

No reply just more singing.

"Hello!" louder this time.

The old man slowly opened his eyes, nodded his head, and motioned for Yeshua to join him by patting the ground next to him. "This is a good place. The rock gives us shade all day. As the sun moves we just move a little bit to keep up with it."

"It is yet morning. The sun is in the east."

"Why, yes it is. You are a smart boy."

"Who were you singing to?" Yeshua joining the old man in the shade.

"Oh, I was just singing to Yahweh, to the rock, and to myself."

"Why?"

"It is pleasing to Yahweh and to me." After a brief pause, "You know Yahweh?"

Yeshua nodded, although shyly.

"You are a good boy. I will sing to you. You tell me if I sing something you know."

The song had a certain rhythm that became predictable. Sometimes the old man would sway. Yeshua would sway with him.

"I know that story! That is the story of Abraham! My mother has told me about Father Abraham." Yeshua a little pleased with himself.

"Yes, yes. You are a good boy. You must come to this

rock whenever you want to. I come here every day. I will sing to you as well as Yahweh and this rock."

"We will shift around now so we can stay in the shade. Do you see how the sun is sneaking up on your legs?" After they resettled, the old man shared bits of cheese with Yeshua. A sip of water would have been nice.

After a few days of long absences his mother questioned him about his whereabouts.

"I know of this old man," said father. "Some say he was a Rabbi, others say he was a priest. They say he sits out by that big rock and recites the scriptures. Although no one can say for sure where he came from. Supposedly he became too old to perform his duties, and having no fortune of his own, was put out." All this in response to his mother's worry that Yeshua had been away from home far too long and had reported this to his father. "The old man is harmless. The boy can visit with him when he likes."

Turning to Yeshua, "This old man deserves respect. You must bring food and drink when you see him. Take that goat skin for water when you visit him." Turning to mother, "I will buy you another skin for the house. The boy can take a small bit of cheese or bread when he goes."

"So do you see what I mean gentlemen? We cannot say where his spiritual journey began. Was it with his father's protection, his mother's love or her stories? Or was it with the old man by the rock?"

Those days and weeks with the old man by the rock were one of Yeshua's fondest memories. He often told me this as we walked along. He taught Yeshua to sing the recitations. Sometimes Yeshua would sing for me.

"You know," the old man said to Yeshua, "These young priests today have to sit with the scrolls in order to do justice to the scriptures. They need the scrolls to remind them where they are in the story. I only need this, as he pointed to his head, and this, as he pointed to his heart." Yeshua told me that the old man was usually full of quiet wisdom and a readiness to teach and showed pride only on this one occasion.

It was the only time he ever boasted of his memory. That's why Yeshua remembered it. It was a funny thing for the old man to say. But I can tell you; Yeshua needed no scrolls as he sang to me along the way. We didn't have scrolls anyway. Besides the sheep liked it.

But, Phillip, why do you say this was a journey with no children?

Ah, Mark, that is a good question. I will tell you what transpired between Yeshua and the old man at the rock.

"I have a brother and a sister," Yeshua said as he began sharing more and more with the old man.

"Yes, I know."

"The other families, they have no children."

"Oh, they have children. Some of the children died when they were very young. Others have been sold as slaves to the people in the cities because their families are too poor to care for them. There is work in some of the fields. It is hard labor. The children work along side of the men."

"Do they ever play or climb trees or hear stories?"

"Well, they may hear stories from time to time. Everyone likes to hear a good story. But play? Climb trees? No," shaking his head slowly from side to side.

"If it was me I would get enough money from my work so I could go home. Then I could hear my mother's stories all the time and be with my family all the time."

The old man pondered for a long time. This young boy, this Yeshua, had depth. He could tell from the questions. And yet he was still an innocent child. When he sensed the long silence had become too much for the youngster at his side, he responded. "The men take their wages. The parents take their wages. The children never get any money. They are lucky to get one meal a day. Many die." This was said in a quiet prayer-like tone. Meant to educate, not to inspire fear.

Yeshua got up from his place in the shade and wandered around the rock. Now kicking dirt. Now looking at the sun. Looking at the sky. He circumnavigated the big rock, not actually counting the number of times he went around.

Yeshua sat back down with the old man and asked, "Doesn't Yahweh care about the children?"

For the next several days Yeshua did not return to the rock. The story of the enslaved children bothered him so. He occupied his time by sitting in the doorway of his home, a big stick at his side. No one was going to take his brother or sister away. He wondered if his parents worried about anyone taking him away.

"Yeshua, you have been sitting in the doorway for two days. You have been underfoot, especially when your father has gone."

"I am guarding my family."

"And why do you think we need this protection?"

"I don't know. Maybe someone bad will come."

"I don't think anyone is coming. Besides, your father is an important man in the village now. He has friends here. No one will harm us."

The next day with the old one at the big rock.

"I don't have enough money to buy back all those children." More a question to the old man than a statement.

"No."

"We all have a special purpose, don't we?"

"Yes."

"What is my purpose?"

"I think you are beginning to discover it, a little at a time. Come. Close your eyes. No more thinking now. No more worry. I will sing for you. Then we will eat. I have some grapes."

Someone adjusted the lamp. Phillip had given us much to think about, to ponder. No one spoke. There was a long silence. The listeners were gathering in this information about the leader who they missed so. Even when he was very young he was very wise. It is no wonder he had a special place for children in his heart. He even let the children sit on his lap and tug at his beard at the end of a long tiring day with the multitudes.

Excuse us for drifting off into our own thoughts, Phillip. We have not heard these stories of his childhood. This gives us pause to consider many of the things he taught us.

Shall I tell you of his trip back to this place, Mark?

Yes. Have some refreshment and continue. Please.

"I have enough money. After Shabbat we will go," said Yosuf.

"Husband, do you think that is wise? What about Yeshua and well, . . . you know."

"We will be well. We will return to family and old friends. That king has long since died. The danger has passed. I am sure of it."

"Our children are safe here. We have a home here. You have work. It is such a long walk back."

"We have been blessed. Yahweh has protected us. Yeshua must have a tutor. The children must grow up with other children. It will be good to be with family again. I have enough money. After Shabbat we will go. We will go by boat."

"Boat?"

"You have walked a long way carrying my children in your belly. This time you will not have to walk. We will trade salt spray for dust. I will work to pay for our passage. I have arranged this with the boat owner. You must keep the children out from under foot. I will not be able to watch out for them."

It was a two-day walk to get to the boat. Miriam was a bit anxious. Sometimes to the point of being fearful, but she never faltered.

When the boats finally came in sight Yeshua's father led them across some planks and onto the boat that was to carry them. This boat and the other boats around it were not as large as Yeshua had imagined. But the openness of the water was vast. You could see to the end of the earth. He said his mother put on a brave face as she followed behind supervising the children, but she didn't fool Yeshua.

"Home," was all she could say.

Yeshua only knew one small dusty village as home. He did not understand his mother's nostalgia; he could only feel a sense of adventure at the upcoming voyage.

The Journey With No Compassion

Phillip, your words are most interesting. You have already alluded to a second journey. Can you tell us of this? We can go up to the roof where it is cooler.

Sitting on the roof is a good suggestion, Mark. When we get settled I can continue the story in the evening cool.

The second time he went to sea held none of the idyllic memories or any of the pleasant experiences of the first. That first voyage took them along the coast. Sunrise and sunset were not to be missed. Beautiful! The coast was almost always in sight. He could wander around the small boat. Smells were of land and water and leather goods and fish and wet rope. Sometimes he would hold Father's tools when Father was working on the boat. Sometimes he would bring food to the sailors. More fun than work.

At the end of the voyage was another walk. But this walk took days and days. Not because of the distance, but because they stopped for a time to stay with people that Yosuf knew. They would have food. There were children to run with. Stories and laughter would go on into the evening. Then they would be off again sometimes for only a short walk as they stopped again for a day or two. Thus was their journey repeated until the family arrived at Nazareth.

When they got to Nazareth there were people to meet. There as everywhere since they left the boat, people would greet them and look upon Yeshua with smiles, some tearful, as blessings were said. They would fondly ruff up the hair on his head and otherwise tell him he was a good boy. Others just looked at him and smiled. Mother presented his brother and sister at each event. But at each event she didn't need to present Yeshua. Some how, some way that he couldn't readily figure out, they all knew him.

Apparently his father had sent ahead some money and instructions. For when they finally reached Nazareth a modest dwelling was awaiting them. Here mother danced and twirled around their one big open room with arms outstretched and tears in her eyes. She soon had to sit for she was with child again. But she was happy. She was home. Blessings were said.

Just when Yeshua had begun to feel comfortable in Nazareth with his new friends his father had some interesting but puzzling news for him. Yeshua was running with children who were younger by several years. Boys his own

age were already working. Some were working with wealth-
ier family others working along with their own fathers. The
older boys he only saw on Shabbat. Yeshua had never been
sent to work. The times he had worked along side his father
had been fun, although Yeshua had the feeling at such times
that his father wanted to keep a closer watch over him
rather than teach him a trade. The news was this: Yeshua
would go to study with a local rabbi. Interesting because he
was not being sent to work but to study. Puzzling because
study was for the sons of the wealthy and the priests. How
would his father pay for this he wondered?

Yeshua remembered his father taking him aside for a
private talk. "Yeshua, I have seen Rabbi Isaac. He has
agreed to tutor you in the scriptures and other matters."

"I know the scriptures, I sang with the old man by the
rock." He really liked his freedom and wasn't sure what
studying with a rabbi meant. But the only thing he could
think to say was singing by the rock. Then he thought of
money. "How will you pay for it?" Yeshua wanted to know.

"You will live with the rabbi. You will rise early each
day and make ready the places of the other scholars. You
will do errands and deliver messages for the rabbi. At the
end of each day you will tidy up and see to it that all is in
order to the rabbi's satisfaction. In this way you will pay for
a portion of your studies. I will give the rabbi a little money
to pay for the rest. When you are home with your mother
you will teach what you have learned to your brother. That
is how we will pay for it." The sternness in his father's voice
had settled it.

We were not told of any schooling. Yet it seems impossible now to think in any other way. Of course he had to have some kind of training. It's what set him apart from the zealots and the revolutionaries. I'm sorry I interrupted, Phillip, it's just that this is all so new . . . and meaningful. Please continue.

I don't mind the interruptions. We have a cool breeze here on the roof. It is pleasant enough for me to continue.

Now, time for Yeshua seemed to slow down. No more running with the other children. Life began to have more serious tones. A full night's sleep was rare for the rabbi was up late and rose early. The days at week's end were especially frantic for Yeshua because he still had to complete all his duties and still get home before sundown.

On one such home visit Yeshua said to his father, "You know the end of the age is near?"

"I have heard much talk of this. Some say there will be a Great War lead by a messenger from Yahweh. Others are not so sure. If it is true I would hate to be a Roman. If it is not true I guess life will go on. What does your rabbi say?"

"He says a messiah will come on a great war horse and rally all of Yahweh's people into a great army in order to scatter the Romans to the far corners of the earth."

"And what are your thoughts?"

"I am not sure what to think. The other scholars believe in this war and seem ready to fight the Romans. Their fathers, so they say, only go along with the Romans in order to keep the peace for the people. But when the messiah comes they will be ready to do Yahweh's bidding."

"And will you fight in such a war?"

"No. They talk of their fathers working along side of the Romans. But isn't it those very positions that creates their wealth? Don't the priests take money from the people, too? It seems that the people have more enemies than just the Romans."

"Have you said this to Rabbi Isaac? Did you tell them what you think?"

"No. I don't talk much. Mostly they act like I am not there. I have things to do for the rabbi while they are discussing scholarly matters. I listen, though, very hard. Sometimes Rabbi Isaac and I talk in the evenings when the others have gone. He seems different when we are alone. Not so guarded. I think he is afraid of what some of the scholars will say to their fathers. So I just do my duties and listen."

"Hmm, yes, well, that is wise I think," Yosuf told him.

Ah, but to the second voyage that you asked about. Yes, Yeshua told me about that second voyage. I can still hear the excitement in his voice as he told me. You see, this voyage rescued him from his studies and taught him more about the world than Rabbi Isaac could teach him. Another boat trip would be a great event.

This time it was only Yeshua and his father. Mother and the children stayed at home. This was a business trip. A chance to make money. He was now in the world of trading and traveling. No more dusty villages. No more frantic days with Rabbi Isaac. Only guilt. Mother was quite opposed to this journey. Father said that the Romans would be building again. That would mean a need for tools, leather, rope, finery for the women they will bring along with them. A man

who was prepared for such events could make a profit. A
man must teach his son how to get along in the world. They
would go in spite of Miriam's objections. No dust. Only
guilt.

So this was his second boat trip, then, Phillip?

Yes, it was, and he found the master of the boat to be a hard
man. He had little concern for the merchants aboard and
even less concern for his own men who worked the sails
and the oars. The sailors worked without rest, especially in
rough seas. Father had traded his labor for their passage. Father wanted to use his money to purchase goods to trade
with the Romans at home. So he worked. The other merchants just sat. They sat atop their merchandise and kept a
wary eye on the sailors and the other merchants. They sat
and ate cheese and olives and guarded what was theirs.

Father worked hard. The boat was old. He was always
patching or repairing. It was difficult to work when the sea
rolled and the cargo shifted and the boat master shouted in
a strange tongue. Still father worked. He had made a bargain and he would work for their passage. Yeshua worked
along with him. They had only their personal affects and
their food to guard. The others were untrusting and kept to
themselves. He told me that conversations, when they occurred, were short, but with an edge to them. The men
spoke in accents that were hard to understand.

For some reason Yeshua remembered back to when he
and Levi had a conversation by the oasis when Yeshua was
a little boy on his way to Egypt. The conversation was about

mean people and nice people. The men on the boat triggered the memory, I think.

"Mean people, like that camel driver over there, are no good," Levi told him. "He is almost evil my father says. He strikes his camel, he strikes his wife, and he strikes his slave all in the same mean way. Best to avoid him and people like him. Nice is like your mother. She smiles and is friendly."

Nice he understood. Mean and evil were foreign to him, then as now. Not until this boat trip did he begin to really understand. To show you what I mean I will relate to you an event on this boat that stood out in Yeshua's mind.

"Yeshua. Yeshua. I am talking to you."

"Yes, father." His father had interrupted his thoughts, you see.

"I need your help here, aren't you listening?"

"Sorry father, I was thinking."

"Thinking! Always thinking." His father said that softly, almost under his breath. But Yeshua still heard him. Louder now, " Go get my chisel. I can't make this bench right until I have my chisel."

Fetching a chisel was a normal request from his father. Up he bounded and away he went to get the chisel from among their belongings. In his zeal to make up for his daydreaming he bounced off a sailor who was making his way forward. The sailor shouted something vile and then swung a fist in Yeshua's direction. Whether the sailor intended his punch to miss or whether it just missed is something Yeshua would never know. But miss it did. Yeshua just stood there open-mouthed as the sailor gave out a laugh with his head cocked back then continued on his way. Shaking off his

amazement that someone would actually strike him in anger
he remembered the chisel but proceeded more cautiously. At
the place in the boat where their belongings were stored
Yeshua bent to retrieve the chisel. As he was feeling around
in the tools a shout reached his ears. Shouts were by now
common but this one seemed to be directed at him. One of
the merchants had taken it upon himself to berate Yeshua.
Of his particular crime Yeshua was unaware as the shouts
came in a language not easily understood. But it seemed
that the merchant thought Yeshua was stealing from among
his goods. When Yeshua produced the chisel and showed it
to the merchant, the merchant immediately backed off and
became quiet.

"What took you so long? I have been waiting." His father wanted to know.

As Yeshua began to relate his recent encounters with
the sailor and with the merchant, father ceased his work
and listened intently.

"So, you think everyone is nice like your mother? You
have entered the world of men. You must act like a man."

"But why did the merchant look so scared when I
showed him the chisel?"

"You showed him the chisel so he would know you
were getting a tool for your father and not stealing from
him?"

"Yes."

"But he is from the world of men. He thought you were
going to attack him with that chisel."

"But father, I would never. . . . Why would he even
think that?"

"He would think that because he has himself been attacked in that manner before. He would think that because
he thought you were a thief and you would stab him as you
tried to get away. He would think that because he would use
such a tool as a weapon against someone else. Who knows
why he would think that? This is the world of men."

"The world of men is a harsh place."

"It can be."

Yes, the world of men was a ponderous thing for
Yeshua. He recalled the time in Jerusalem when he went
into the temple. Men were not so harsh. It was Passover. His
family, including aunts, uncles, cousins, and friends would
frequently travel together into Jerusalem each year at the
time of Passover. He was now of age to go into the temple
with the men and sit and discuss scripture. Wasn't this the
world of men? In years passed Passover was more fun than
serious. He got to run and play and gawk at all of the visi-
tors. As long as he was quiet and respectful at the various
meals his family pretty much left him alone. But now he
could sit in with the men who were wearing fine robes and
singing from scrolled parchment. He could listen to the de-
bates. He could hear the discourse of important and re-
spected men. He remembered he had stayed for days.

"How does such a young scholar come to us?" the men
wondered. "With whom did you study?"

"Rabbi Isaac," was the answer.

"I do not know this Rabbi Isaac. Still he must be very
proud of such a fine scholar. You seem to know the usual
stories and can recite the law, which many your age cannot
do. But you know the prophets as well. And you speak with

a certain authority not found in someone so young. You are truly favored."

It was about this time that his father had burst in. He could hear his mother's voice calling from out side, almost crying, his name.

"Where have you been? What have you been doing?" Father did not seem to hear the praise and admiration in the voices of the surrounding men.

"There you are, father. I thought you knew where I was. I thought you left me here so I could learn from these men."

"Let's go, Yeshua!" very firmly but still respectful of where they were. "Your mother is beside herself with worry," his father said in a loud trying-to-be-discreet whisper. Turning to those assembled Yosuf said, "Thank you, gentlemen, for indulging my son." And out they went.

"Yeshua, Yeshua, have you eaten? What have you been doing? Don't you know that we have been worried?" Mother was crying and laughing at the same time. She stroked his cheek lovingly.

The scolding from his father continued all of the way out of the city. Looking at him out of the corner of his eye father would scold some more. Mother kept her arm around his shoulder all the way through the gate.

"Which is the true world of men?" he wondered "The world of boats, and distrust, and violence or the world of debate, and the law, and love?" He knew this was not the time to discuss such matters with his father. He knew also that this was not the place. "Maybe Levi was right. Maybe there were just mean people and nice people."

But I am afraid that the harshness returned. He said

they could smell the smell long before they reached the city. A land breeze was carrying a disgusting stench downward along the hill they were walking up. To get to the city meant walking along the road uphill. The boats lay anchored behind them. Carts were passing them on the road down to the boats. The carts would be hired to carry goods up the hill.

Yeshua asked a passing cart driver, "What is that awful smell?"

"Humph," was the only answer

"Father, what is that awful smell?"

"I am not sure. But if it is what I think it is, then it will not be pleasant."

The source of the stench appeared as the hill began to level off. Some men were suspended from wooden posts. Others were tied to wooded frames built up from the hillside. Large birds were perched on the posts and on the men themselves. The birds were pecking at the flesh. None of the men had eyes. The birds had apparently pecked out the eyes first and were now working on the flesh. Dogs lazed in the shade of the hillside, wary and removed from the traffic on the road. Ever vigilant for a quick scrap of meat.

Yeshua took all of this in with one profound look. His senses were overcome. He wretched. Yeshua realized that these things were no longer men but dead bodies hanging from wooden frames.

"Father, why do they hang dead bodies in this way?"

"They were not dead when they were put there. They were put there to die."

"Who would do such a thing?"

"The Romans."

"Why?"

"I cannot say for sure. Perhaps they were robbers or criminals. Perhaps they were slaves who fought against their masters. So they had to die in this way. It is not good to defy Roman law. . . . These bodies are here for all to see and be reminded. The Romans will keep the peace at any cost. . . . If you still must know we will find out in the city."

One such criminal was still alive. He was moaning and moving his head from side to side in endless sun-beaten agony. There were people gathered at his feet who were handing up food with sticks, one stick had a water skin fastened to it. When they were not keeping him thus nourished, they used the same sticks to keep the birds away.

As travelers along the road would pass by he would summon his strength and shout curses. He would curse the Romans. He would curse the governor. Then he would lapse again into his crucified agony.

"Father, how long do you think he has been hanging there?"

The answer came not from his father but from a Roman soldier who, up until this time, had remained unnoticed. "Five days."

"Five days!"

"The strong ones, or the stubborn ones, can last that long, provided the birds and the dogs don't eat them. But this one. This one has food and drink. He will last at least another day, maybe two. They should let him die. But they think like he does. If they are not careful they will end up the same way."

Rising above the smell of decaying bodies that permeated his nostrils and shedding his surprise at seeing the soldier, Yeshua asked, "Why does he curse so?"

"He hates all that is Roman."

"Surely a powerful hate."

The soldier held Yeshua in his gaze. "Be careful young man what you say."

Inside the city Yosuf seemed to be looking for something.

"Father, what are you looking for?"

"I will know it when I see it"

Toward the end of the day the two of them came upon a small gathering of men. Yeshua had never seen these men before, he was sure of that. Yet they were familiar in some way. As father approached them they ceased their talking and addressed him. Their conversation went on for some moments before father said his thanks to them and rejoined Yeshua who had been taking in the sights of this new city.

"Do you know those men, father?"

"No, I have never met them before. But I knew such men as these must be about somewhere in this city. They are our people. They are like you and me."

"They know Yahweh?"

"Yes. They told me where we should sleep while we are here. There will be a small gathering to observe Shabbat. And I know of a place where we can get food this evening. Fresh food would be good after a long boat ride, yes?"

"Yes, but how did you know they would be here?"

"We are everywhere in every land. We don't just live in

Jerusalem you know. Didn't you learn about that from your old friend by the rock and from Rabbi Isaac?"

"So the stories are true?"

"There is much wisdom in the old stories," his father told him. "The rest you have to figure out for yourself. . . . It is good to know you have people you can rely on when you are away from home. But always you must rely on your own judgment."

The gathering of men occurred at a large house that was built around a courtyard. The house was the largest one Yeshua had ever been in. It was big enough to surround a courtyard. The courtyard itself was much bigger even than his own home in Nazareth. The courtyard held many men dressed in all sorts of clothing, some rich looking some ordinary. By all appearances, the one common thread that held them together was that they were all some sort of merchant.

Torches supplied the light. In the torch light Yeshua recognized one of the merchants from the boat. Thereafter he kept a wary eye out for the one who had yelled at him. Tables supported trays of food in the form of fruit and meat. All eaten with the fingers.

Yeshua sampled a few olives and grapes before he was bold enough to sample a type of food he had not yet encountered. The sweet taste tingled in his mouth. The savory sweetmeat was surely a delicacy reserved for the privileged. The sweetmeat seemed to make his taste buds smile.

"Yeshua, come here!" Father's tone was quiet but demanding. " I am wondering why we should be invited here. Make your way back to where we came in. I will mingle and then meet you on the way out. Eat little, drink nothing."

"But there is nothing to drink."

"If I am right I think there will be . . . very shortly."

Yeshua made his way quickly back toward the gate. The gate was manned by a slave, but Yeshua did not talk to him. He watched his father walk slowly through the crowd. Now and then father would speak with some of the merchants. Sometimes father would just listen. When slave girls emerged from the shadowy torchlight carrying pitchers and goblets, father headed directly for Yeshua. They left immediately.

"Why did we go there if we weren't going to stay to eat and drink? I sure would like another taste of that sweetmeat."

"What you have just seen is a very dishonorable way to trade. The owner of the house will provide wine into the night. Many bad bargains will be made tonight because of the drink. Some men will awake in the morning to discover that their goods have been stolen. Others will not be allowed to leave until they have paid for the slave girl they were provided for the night."

"Father, I don't under . . ."

"You don't understand because you see the world as your mother sees it! There are people who will rob you, trick you . . . all to gain an advantage over you. Your mother is all smiles and singing. She bears children, seeks happiness and contentment. In the world of men you must be wary of those with cold hearts who would steal from you."

"Were you told of this place by those men we met today?"

"Yes."

"And were they not Jews who know the law?"

His anger and bitterness now peaking, father just shouted, "What do you think!"

They rose early the next morning offering little thanks for the hospitality they had been shown. They traded only for a few items like metal tools and hammers with strong wooden handles. These they could carry themselves.

"We will walk toward the east", his father told him. "We will trade and work as we make our way home. We may have to ride in a boat or two for short distances. Hopefully, we will meet up with a caravan going south toward home and your mother and new brother or sister."

"Surely the baby will not be born for another few months."

"It will take that long, or longer, to get home."

In fact, it took them a few days short of fifteen weeks to get home. There were actually three times they made use of a boat. Twice by necessity and once out of convenience.

They carried the new tools, father's tools, and their food in sacks that slung over their shoulders. The first few days were cumbersome but they soon fell into a routine with conversation ebbing and flowing. Yeshua was also beginning to show signs of a beard. A fact that father chose to tease him about from time to time. "Your mother will not recognize you with that hairy face" or "The girls will not want such a man with a scratchy beard."

As they purchased more goods their burdens became harder to bear. Yeshua felt himself grow into the challenge of carrying a man's burden in the world of men. Father finally relented and bought a cart. Now they took turns pushing the cart because father was not ready yet to trade for a donkey. The cart was a different type of burden. For while the cart held all of their goods, it need only to be pushed by one man. Yeshua began to take a larger share of the day pushing and sometimes pulling the cart. Help was needed on severe inclines and declines; otherwise Yeshua could push it himself.

I remember one place he recalled for me where they stopped to trade. The mood there appeared festive. But appearances did not always tell the whole story. There were people about selling food; it seemed in the populated areas these were always around. But here there were people involved in games of running and of strength as well. The entertainers attracted large crowds like bees to honey. While on the one hand people engaged in such activities Yeshua was aware that on the other hand these same people did not seem to be enjoying themselves. He recalled the exhilaration of running with the other children back home. How it was fun just to run. These runners were not having fun.

"Father, it is an exciting time here. But there is something else happening here that I do not understand."

"On the surface the presence of games, and food, and magicians, and competitions should make for exciting times. But, did you know that the winner of the race gets a prize and honor for his birthplace and his family? All of the others can only earn disgrace. If you do not win you may not be welcome at home after the competitions are over.

"You see those men over there? They are gathering wagers of money for the next race. These competitions are a way to earn honor or money. It is a serious business. Not fun. It is like a war where there are no armies, only athletes and gamblers."

Yeshua and his father then flowed along with the crowds watching the events or trying to figure out how the magician made those coins disappear or how he found the coins behind someone's ear or in his other hand. But the healer was an event unto himself. Not many people were gathered over there by the healer. Those who were congregating near him looked bedraggled, one or two had a crutch for support. Occasionally someone in the crowd would yell an insult toward the healer. Other negative comments were directed at the infirm. But mostly the healer and his unwell followers were ignored by the crowds.

Yeshua felt himself being pulled in the direction of the healer by an unknown force. He had had this feeling before and learned to give in to it. So he asked, "Father, what is happening over there?"

"Those people? Those people have come in hopes that the healer will cure them. They bring money and beg for his attention. The healer then takes their money and offers a potion or a prayer or a ritual for a cleansing of their infirmity. He is worse than a thief. The people are desperate to be healed and he gladly takes their money. Only he makes it seem like an honorable transaction. At least that magician back there makes no pretense of fooling people. Everyone knows it is a trick. Just try to figure out the trick. But when you deal with a healer such as this one you are tricked by your own mind. You have to believe you were healed because you have paid money. A true healer, one who heals with authority, takes no money. A true healer does not profit from the agony of others. But he rejoices in the healing."

Yeshua looked up at his father with renewed admiration. Even in the world of men strong men like his father could be wise, and compassionate.

Yeshua did not remember much of what happened after they met the healer. He remembered that they watched for a while but became melancholy over all of the illness and went on their way. Yeshua continued to ponder what his father had told him and what he saw. He remembered thinking, "If you could heal someone wouldn't you just heal them? And if you couldn't heal them why would you take their money and say you could?"

He didn't remember eating. He barely recollected when his father purchased the donkey. He continued to brood over his fathers words, the duplicity of the healer, and the power he felt budding in his own inner soul. Everything else on that day was just murky memory.

Yes, Phillip, I can believe it. He was on his spiritual journey even then. He was growing into a man and growing in the spirit also. Permit me to get you a hot drink before you continue.

Thank you for the tea. . . . The journey was not all melancholy, you know. There were conversations to be had and more lessons to learn. Listen as these events unfold.

"This donkey reminds me of when you were born," Yosuf had said absently.

His father had purchased a donkey to pull the cart. They

need not carry the goods themselves or push the cart themselves. The donkey did a major part of the work. They still carried some of the goods in sacks slung over their backs in order to lighten the load on some of the steep inclines. But the hilly country was mostly behind them now. So they did not have to carry goods very often now.

"We have had other donkeys before, you know," Yosuf continued his mutterings. "Ah, yes. But this one looks much like the one your mother rode when she was carrying you inside her."

Yeshua had heard the story surrounding his birth told many times through the years. The more distant the relative, the greater the story was embellished. However, this was the one and only time father had ever mentioned it. Yeshua did not interrupt or say anything to change the subject. He wanted his father to continue.

"Did she ride donkeys when she bore the other children?"

"No." Yeshua had anticipated this answer. He had heard the story often enough to know the order of events. But he wanted to keep his father talking. Father rarely shared such intimate insights.

"Then why was she riding? Where were you going?"

"You have not heard your aunts and your cousins speak of this?"

"Yes. But never from you."

After a pause of some moments, Yosuf drifted into the story as they trekked on. "I had to return to the land of my birth because the Romans wanted to count people. Count people! If you could imagine! The Romans, always the Romans. I think it was more about squeezing more tax money out of the people. But, any way I had to go. Your mother was in no condition to walk her time being so close. So I got her a donkey. Not that riding on a donkey was any more comfortable for a mother about to give birth. Still, she had a choice. So she walked some and rode when she was tired.

"I was concerned that you were going to be born somewhere along the road side. So was your mother. She was even more worried about who would help her with the birth. There were many people out and about on the roads in those days. Would one of them be a midwife when the time had come?

"But we got there in due time. We arrived a day later than I thought we would. Travel was slow. Both your mother and the donkey needed rest. We were late. Many others had already arrived and taken up all the rooms. Some were sleeping in the streets. Others had brought tents and slept out beyond the inhabitants."

Father was silent for a while as he recalled the events. Yeshua did not break the silence.

"The room I had arranged for was taken. The owner wanted to insure himself a profit so he rented out our room because we were not there at the appointed time. I thought I had a room waiting so I did not think to bring a tent. I could not allow your mother to sleep in the street when she was so near to her time. I bargained with an innkeeper to use his stable. Others had tried for the stable as well. But I prevailed because I told him I would also care for his animals and sweep out the stable. He was not overly concerned that your mother was near her time, but he did offer information about a woman who sometimes helped in the birthing of babies and animals as well.

"So after I cleared away and rearranged and got your mother and our donkey settled. I went in search for this woman. I found her where the innkeeper said I would. I told her that your mother was about to deliver and asked would she come quickly. She said, 'Quickly, what do men know?' But she came. You were born that night. The midwife smacked you a good one when you came out of your mother's womb. But you didn't cry like babies do. You gulped some air and then snuggled at your mother's breast where you took comfort. The not crying part I did not see. I was not allowed to watch the actual birth. I don't think the midwife was very fond of men. Your mother told me that part later, and why should she make up such a thing?

"Anyway, word spread around that crowded town that a baby had been born in a stable. Having no entertainments and needing some diversion from the Romans, people came by to see this baby who was just born. At first I tried to shoosh them away. But your mother insisted that I let her show you off."

The reverie of the quiet story telling was broken by a shout from beyond a large rock ahead. Another shout as if in answer came from behind them. "Hold. We will have your goods. Maybe if you give up your goods peaceably we will let you live."

"Robbers! I had not heard that there were robbers in this country. Be prepared for anything. We may have to fight for our lives."

As startled as they were by the robbers, the robbers, in

turn, were startled by a contingent of Roman soldiers on horseback. The robbers were soon scattered. Yeshua never did learn how many robbers there were. The soldiers killed one, captured one, and said the others must have fled. They wanted to know how many robbers there were. Father could only account for the two voices they heard.

The officer in charge dismounted and spoke to father. After that he inspected the cart. He located a fine silk scarf that father was hoping to make a good profit on. He stuffed the scarf inside his tunic.

"Where are you going?" More a demand than a question.

"My son and I are headed home to the east and then to the south of this country."

"Don't you know you should be traveling in groups this far out? There is strength in numbers you know."

"We had not heard that there were robbers here about."

"Now you know for sure. . . . Yesterday we made contact with a caravan headed south. You are a day behind. But if you travel hard and escape any more bandits you may join up with them and in so doing arrive home safely. . . . I have inspected your cart. You owe Rome a road tax for a two wheeled cart pulled by a donkey."

Father paid the tax.

The Roman contingent went one way and Yeshua and his father went the other. Father grumbling. "Taxes always the taxes."

"Father, the soldiers chased the robbers away. You paid the tax."

"Has anyone else charged us a road tax these many days?"

"No. But we are still alive. And just for a little tax money."

"And the scarf. Don't forget the scarf!"

So, they became very selective that night as to where to make their camp. They passed by several depressions deep enough to hide the cart and donkey from view in tomorrow's morning sunlight. They kept pushing on, eager to join up with the caravan. On a decline they came to a carved out section of rock. It wasn't deep enough to call a cave, but it was a good place to defend. Since it was improbable that they would find anything better in the coming darkness they decided, well, Yosuf decided that this was as good as any a place they were likely to find.

The donkey was unhitched from the cart and led in first. Yeshua and his father muscled the cart in sideways across the entrance. No fire that night. Cold food for them and what little they could gather for the donkey. The donkey licked moisture from the rock wall. The men had no water. Father slept atop the cart, Yeshua underneath. They each had a hammer and a chisel to use as weapons if they needed.

As he waited for sleep to come, Yeshua realized that he never knew where his father slept during that first caravan trip into the land of Egypt. Yeshua and his mother slept under the protection of a leather tent father fashioned to the side of the cart. Mother pushed Yeshua in close to where the leather was fastened to the ground, covering him with a rug. She slept between Yeshua and the opening wrapped in her robe. Father must have been atop the cart or outside the tent. He remembered that riding in that cart had not been all that comfortable. He couldn't imagine sleeping there.

The only reason they were able to catch up to the caravan at all was because the caravan had halted. When they were in sight of the caravan and the caravan in sight of them two riders came out to meet them. It was not a friendly greeting. Both riders had weapons drawn.

"Who is the leader of this caravan?"

"Levi is the caravan master."

"That is good news. Take me to Levi. We are not robbers. We ourselves have been attacked, but were rescued by Roman soldiers."

"We have not been so lucky. We were attacked yesterday. We are just now regrouping to find out the extent of the damage and the thievery. I am afraid we have a few dead. You may be able to replenish our numbers. If Levi takes you in."

"Yes, well, he will take us."

Levi walked out to meet them. The outriders had informed Levi that the two newcomers desired to join the caravan. They did not appear to have evil intent. So Levi walked out to meet them and take their measure for himself. When he was close enough to recognize father he broke into a big smile.

"Well, old friend. I see that you get around a little. And who is this? Is this your son? Yes, it is your son. I can see that." Addressing Yeshua he said, "I remember that you and I had many nice talks all those years ago."

Yeshua had no recognition of who this was talking to

him. He seemed to know his father and his father was not alarmed so it must be all right.

Seeing the uncertainty on Yeshua's face Levi asked him, "Which way is north?"

Yeshua pointed north with stirrings of recognition.

"How do you know which way is north?" his inquisitor wanted know.

"I know because the rising sun is there. When I put my face to the rising sun north is on my left." And with full realization that this was the shepherd boy who had taught him his directions he said, "At night I can look for the north star as it appears thus." Yeshua pointed to where the North Star would be this very evening.

"You remember," Levi said with some pleasure. "That is good. But now to the business at hand: you have overtaken us in a state of some confusion. We were attacked and looted yesterday by a ragtag group of bandits. They appeared to be deserters from the Roman army and runaway slaves. They were not very disciplined but they managed to conduct their rotten business well enough. They stole what goods they could ride off with. One man died trying to save his slave girl from being taken. They scattered our herds and killed the shepherd." Showing his anger now, "Take some animals for meat I can understand. But kill the shepherd? Madness."

Settling down to the business at hand Levi continued, "That was yesterday's business. " Gesturing that they should walk with him back toward the caravan Levi said, "Today we must gather together what we have and resume our journey. We need carts repaired, sheep and goats gathered in, extra hands to help conduct us on our way." It was not the boy Yeshua remembered who was doing the talking; it was the man he had grown into. "Yosuf," being very decisive, "You will help repair the carts. Your son will gather what sheep and goats he can find."

"He is no longer a boy, but a man. He will decide himself what he will do."

Levi appraising Yosuf quickly but not missing a step turned to Yeshua, "Yeshua, I need you to gather what sheep and goats you can find. Being a shepherd for a caravan is not very glamorous work. There are those who even though they went through the fight yesterday, will not gather the animals today. They know our need and still they will not do it. They feel they are too important for such lowly work. Are you too important, Yeshua?"

Bargaining for work in the world of men was more difficult than he first had imagined. Father had always made it seem so easy. Father's skills were easily identifiable. Their worth recognizable. But to be a young man with unproven skills was another matter. Yeshua could repair the carts as easily as father could. Father had taught him. But there was no need for the both of them to repair the carts that had been overturned to offer shelter from the raiders.

"I am not so important that I cannot be a shepherd."

Many of us gasped at that point. But Phillip was patient. He paused to give us some time to gather our thoughts and then he continued.

As to the business of being a shepherd, then, "Good!" Levi said. It is settled. You will head out toward the east where we found the dead shepherd. You will gather in what animals you can find. I will send out a rider to check on your safety at sundown. I will send out another rider to check on you after sunrise tomorrow. My plan is to be able to resume the journey in two days. On the second morning fall in behind the caravan with what sheep you can find."

The search for the animals proved to be a trying experience. The animals did not know or trust him. They had been scattered. Some were grazing where they could. Others were just wandering. His first order of business had been to claim the dead shepherd's staff for his own. The shepherd did not smell like those bodies that were crucified by the Romans but he was lifeless nonetheless. He gave up his staff without objection. Some sheep were actually resting near the dead body. Reluctant to move away from their trusted leader.

With the gnarled staff in hand Yeshua gently nudged the sheep into a standing position and began to move them. He wasn't sure what direction he should follow. He only knew that he had the remainder of today and all of tomorrow to find as many of the animals as he could. He kept his eyes and ears open for the cry of sheep . . . his sheep now.

Yeshua's intriguing task was to locate the sheep, remember where the caravan was camped, and watch out for his own safety. The horsemen that Levi would send might find him and they might not.

That first night he had backed his sheep up to a thicket. It was not much protection but it gave the sheep and Yeshua some sense of security. Yeshua slept on the ground with the sheep between himself and the thicket. He learned that night that being a shepherd was more than just watching out for the sheep. He had tried to be so responsible in his new vocation that he had forgotten food and drink for himself. Hungry he bedded down for the night.

The next day was a trying one. You see, with little sleep and no food he rose before the sun making a plan to continue circling to the north and east and then back south to rejoin the caravan. Yeshua was now watchful for water. He needed water himself and was sure that he would find some of the animals in such places.

Food was a different matter. He managed to pick a few dried berries that the birds had left. They were bitter and powdery and did little to abate his hunger. Still it was something. He found himself thinking about those sweetmeats he had tasted so many weeks ago.

His flock began to grow. He found a dry creek bed and followed it. There were occasional trees along the creek and some pools of standing water where he found sheep and goats. His flock increased. He sang quietly to the sheep. Yeshua sang the Psalms like the old man had taught him. The singing seemed to keep the animals settled and provided a meditation for himself as well. Rain gathered in the sky.

He was not hungry now. Hunger appeared to be a thing of the morning. The water along the way proved sufficient for now. He realized that he would need something to eat eventually. His concern now was the gathering rain. He kept the flock to the west side of the creek bed reasoning that if there was a major storm coming and the creek filled with water he wanted to be on the same side as the caravan.

Although rain clouds obscured the setting sun he could feel the sun even though he couldn't actually see it. The sheep could feel it too. Night would soon be upon them and he wanted a safe place, hopefully a more comfortable place than last night, to bed down.

A light rain began to fall. Yeshua found a cave that appeared to have been used before as a hold for animals. There were rocks piled along the entranceway that could easily be built up and taken down to allow for the passing of sheep and goats. The sheep went willingly into the hold appreciating the safe place that their shepherd had found for them. After he had built up the wall he rested on a ledge that was inside the cave above the sheep and nicely out of the rain. Sleep came easily.

Bleating entered his consciousness. The sound seemed far off but woke him nonetheless. He quickly surveyed his flock and sensed no immediate danger. Still the bleating continued. Sheep inside the cave answered the bleating. Sleep became impossible. Yeshua hauled himself out into the rainy night to investigate. He found several sheep that had wandered away and had not been penned up for the night. They now apparently wanted shelter from the rain and safety from the night.

Finding them was easy enough. He followed the sound. Getting them back to the cave was another matter. The falling rain made the night darker. Though the sheep were willing to follow Yeshua could not see where to go. He first let the sheep feel the nudging of his staff. Then he began to sing in a very quiet voice calming the animals and himself. He decided to slowly make his way uphill for that is where he remembered the cave to be. Down hill was toward the creek. So it was uphill that he nudged the sheep. Yeshua didn't believe the sheep could see any better than he did in the dark but by some instinct they arrived at the hold. He was able to dismantle the wall enough to let the sheep jump through to safety. He did this more by touch than sight. Feeling his way along the cave wall he located his ledge. He climbed up settled in, and drifted off to sleep thinking that he didn't really care for the smell of wet sheep.

He thought he would easily locate the caravan on the appointed morning by its dust cloud. But the rain had dampened the earth and kept the dust down. So he continued through with his plan now traveling south in hopes of meeting up with his father and Levi.

A way off to the south he saw a lone figure on horseback. He recognized the imposing outline of Levi against the morning sky. Levi did not ride up. Instead he allowed Yeshua and the flock to approach him.

"Yeshua, Yeshua, where did you get all of those sheep? And goats. We had no goats."

Yeshua gestured to the land back to the north and east.

"You have found more animals than we have lost." Throwing back his head Levi laughed right out loud, "You are a great shepherd indeed." Levi then tossed him a package and a wine skin. "I thought I would find you dead of starvation. Since you are still alive and have brought me many animals you must eat and drink to keep up your strength. The caravan has already departed. Keep that reddish-gray rise of land on your left as you proceed south. We will halt early this evening so you can catch up. Find water along the way as you can. We will butcher some of those goats you have found to raise the spirits of my people. They have been under attack and then under a great deal of stress repairing the damage." Turning his horse and pointing south, Levi rode off laughing and shaking his head, "Yeshua the shepherd, Yeshua the shepherd."

Yeshua did not follow the caravan though. He had a different path to take. With the sun moving toward its overhead position he knew that the earth would dry out. The dust would begin again. So he stayed well to the east so the dust cloud did not settle on him. He liked dust even less than he liked wet sheep. Occasionally he would wander in to the caravan encampment at night when he felt his flock was in a safe resting place. He would talk some with the people. He would eat.

He found that he enjoyed the solitude of a shepherd. He could think. He could sing. But mostly he pondered the events of his life to that point, especially this trip. The boat captain, the merchants, the Romans, the dead, the robbers, his father, and of course, Levi. He thought of them all. The world of men was a harsh place but even these men must exist and survive.

Yeshua could not help but notice on those occasions when he did visit the caravan that there were men who appeared to be jealous of the way Levi apparently favored Yeshua and his father. Other men would talk loudly of the smell of goats when he was near. He felt that he was doing a good thing. Others obviously did not. Still, he would uphold his bargain with Levi and be the shepherd for the caravan, regardless of what others thought.

Levi rode out to greet him one day. It had been several days since Yeshua had visited with his father and the other men of the caravan. "Yeshua, I notice that you do not follow the caravan. You make your own way finding better grazing and water for the animals."

"Yes, and I also keep out of the dust," Yeshua told him.

A wry smile crossed Levi's lips. "We will be coming to the end soon. Yosuf tells me you two will be heading home. You know, a shepherd's share of the caravan's profit is not much. Still you have earned it well. Take ten sheep extra for yourself. If I were you I would take ewes carrying lambs. But I am not you."

"Levi, I have had much time to think."

"Yes, well, most shepherds have plenty of time to think. Some think so much that they go crazy. Are you crazy, Yeshua?"

"No, I am not crazy. I have been thinking about the lying and deception I have seen. I have been thinking that in the world of men there are jealousies and suspicions. There is thievery and death. And here you are offering me an additional share. I am not crazy I just do not understand it all."

"There is much honor in hard work my young friend. You have worked well. You have not taken the bait of those who would provoke you. I am pleased so I give you an extra share."

Yeshua told the caravan master, "You talk like my father. 'A man must be honorable in his trade' he would say. Still where is honor without compassion?"

"In the world of men you must earn your place. Once

you have earned your place, then you can teach them compassion."

Yeshua told me he often considered the words of this caravan master. Those words had a profound effect on him.

The Journey With No End

It was on this third journey that I met Yeshua. But I get ahead of myself. Let me share the events of this journey, as best I can, the way it happened.

His other journeys could be measured in weeks or months. This journey would be measured in years. Levi was leaving, traveling north again. He had lead many caravans by this time bringing back tales of adventure, riches, treachery, and triumph. It had been some years since Yeshua had seen Levi. When Levi appeared and began preparations for a new caravan, Yeshua knew that it was time to go. Somehow he felt that he must be a part of the next caravan Levi was taking north. It was time.

His mother had long since relented in commenting and cajoling about Yeshua's actions. She had, instead, taken on a quiet reserve, an almost peaceful countenance, concerning Yeshua's affairs. She made no objection to this trip. Her husband and sons had work. Her daughters were being considered for marriage. She would have a hand in all of that. This son, this one son, she would not cling to. Would not interfere. This son must find his way.

Yeshua remembered all of this and shared it with me. There is little we did not talk about on those days and nights trekking with the caravan or minding the animals. It was the way his thoughts paraphrased the many conversations he had had with his mother. In his earlier years he remembered those conversations as being motherly, parental. Later the conversations softened and took on a friendlier, more advisory and supportive tone. Mother knew. She had always known. Yeshua had always known, too, really. The question was not in knowing but in knowing what to do.

Levi provided the answer, you see. Yeshua would return to the dusty road of Abraham and Moses with his good friend Levi in the lead. He would seek his God under the stars. He would let Yahweh lead him, let Yahweh define the path his destiny was to take.

So Yeshua departed. Once again taking up the role of the shepherd. Levi offered more socially acceptable positions, positions that would earn him a greater share of the profits along the way. But the role of shepherd suited him. The caravan was large enough that great flocks of sheep were needed. This caravan would travel with extra oxen, donkeys and horses. There were many who would be needed to tend the animals. Yeshua numbered himself among those.

Actually Yeshua left before the caravan ever got started. Levi had gathered a great flock of sheep and goats and had sent Yeshua on ahead. He was to water and graze the flock at a protected pastureland that Levi knew. Yeshua would find it easily. The caravan would catch up with and then pass the flock. Yeshua and the animals would then fall in behind the caravan.

"I hope you have food and drink with you this time," laughed Levi.

Holding up a goatskin Yeshua replied, "I have water and I have some food. I am much better at finding food along the way now." Yeshua threw his friend a warm smile, a wave of the hand and then he was off.

The days at the pastureland were simple. The animals pretty much took care of themselves. Yeshua and the other herdsmen fell into a somewhat friendly routine of minding the sheep and resting together under shade trees during the day and about a campfire during the evening. Hot drinks were consumed at night. That is when the stories would begin.

All of the herdsmen were experienced with animals as well as seasoned caravan travelers. Stories about hard weather, dangerous terrain, and untrustworthy people abounded. Most did not have the aptitude to be merchants or traders of any kind, but they could tell stories. The nomadic life suited them. In spite of the low esteem and low pay, they were content to be herdsmen. They enjoyed the adventure and the steady work. Though they often joked about the lack of female companionship.

Instead of stories in which each tried to outdo the other,

one evening the conversation drifted in a gossipy sort of way toward the subject of Levi himself. It had been Yeshua's turn to settle the sheep in for the evening. He was just returning to camp for a bite to eat when he came upon this conversation. While Yeshua ate his belated meal he listened.

"You know, Levi is not his real name," said one of the animal tenders.

"I have heard this but never heard how it came about," replied another.

"It was back many years ago when Levi's father was still the caravan master, though by then much of the work had fallen to Levi. The priests had assembled upon the return of the caravan demanding a share in the profits. For the temple so they said. You know priests. But his father would not pay."

"I thought you were going to tell us his real name."

"Don't interrupt."

"So Levi's father was furious with the priests. And the priests were not happy with him either. Later, as a new caravan was being assembled outside the city walls of Jerusalem the priests once again demanded payment. This time they wanted a sacrifice of animals and food as the temple's share of all that had been gathered. They brought armed men with them to collect. Levi's father had dealt with ruthless bandits and Roman soldiers and was not intimidated by the temple's little army. He laughed at them. A big laugh like Levi laughs."

The listeners laughed as well, refreshing their hot drinks and searching around for any left over food.

"So when his father turned his back on the temple army

they rushed him and knocked him to the ground. The caravan outriders and Levi himself had come to his father's aid.
He was not hurt but the priests had made their mistake. Almost instantly the little army had been disarmed. Levi,
sword drawn, took the weapons from the temple's men.
They were not being paid enough to engage such seasoned
fighters so they gave up easily. Then Levi did a strange
thing. He took his sword and swiped it at the headgear of all
the priests. He stomped their headdresses into the dust. Others joined in the fun. All the while the priests were shouting
out against this great indignity. Levi could not quiet them so
he drew his knife and cut off the beard of the priest nearest
him."

"How did he do that?"

"He grabbed the beard with one hand and sliced it off
with the other. I am sure that he yanked out as many hairs
as he cut off. All the same the priests became quiet. Especially the one with the painful face. None of them had headgear and one had no beard. They were not looking very
priestly."

Laughter all around.

"So Levi's father embraced him. 'My priest fighter,' he
exclaimed. 'I never liked the name your mother gave you. I
will call you Levi in honor of the priestly clan of Levites.'"
The storyteller by now was recounting the story in several
voices embellishing the laughter and mocking the priests for
all he was worth. "And that, my friends, is how Levi got his
name."

Somehow Yeshua was not surprised. He smiled quietly
to himself. As he finished his meal he thought about those

same priests many years ago that had discussed the scrolls with him. "How could these men, learned in the law," he thought, " be the same who demanded payment like the Romans. Do they not keep themselves pure before the law? Would they allow me once again to discuss the scrolls with them or would they keep me away and say that I am impure because I have long been dirty and dusty? Isn't it the purpose of priests to comfort the people? Surely they should not tax men and otherwise keep worshipers out of the temple." But after a few moments of pondering this unanswered question he allowed his attention to drift back to the stories. He did not tell stories back then but he enjoyed listening.

The first few weeks of pasturing the animals were leisurely and pastoral. Now that they were on the trek north in earnest the pace quickened. The animals were well watered and somewhat fat and minded well enough. Resting places were frequently passed by with only a short stop for water, rather than a day of rest and regrouping. Levi was pushing it. Most people knew why. They had gotten a late start. Levi wanted to get the caravan ahead of any northerly weather if he possibly could. So on they went.

This had been Yeshua's first experience with oxen. They were slow but steady beasts. The larger carts were yoked with two oxen. The small carts with but one. The herdsmen had a cart pulled by two oxen that held all of their collective personal belongings. Each of the animal drivers took a turn minding the cart with the caravan while the others herded the animals. This not only gave each of the herdsmen a bit of relief but also proved to be an effective means of communication. As the herdsmen traded places, messages could be passed along about water stops, directions of travel, places to gather, how many animals would need to be butchered or cut out of the flock for trading along the way.

Yeshua made a habit of observing the oxen when it fell to him to be with the caravan. Oxen were slow, but steady. He was used to the jerky pull of a donkey. The constant need to prod the donkey on, especially with a heavy load. This load was too much for any donkey. One great ox may have done the job, but two yoked together seemed to be the best way. He noticed that on occasion the ox yoked on the right did not always pull. He pulled his fair share on slight inclines but would slack off on more level ground and let his partner pull the load. Yeshua was not sure this is what was actually happening but he kept watch. He thought to himself that he would mention this to the other herdsmen.

"So you think that the ox we generally yoke on the right is lazy?"

"I'm not sure. He pulls going uphill, but on level ground sometimes not at all."

"That happens with oxen. Sometimes if you yoke them on the other side they will work better. It is all a matter of how the oxen work together. Some oxen are very lazy and only pull grudgingly. Once you get them started they finally just plod on. That is why we use oxen and not donkeys or horses. But oxen can be like people you know. Sometimes one dominates the other. We have talked about this ox around the campfire."

"What do the others think?"

"Some think that the right ox is lazy. I don't think so. The ox on the right is older than the one on the left. The one on the left is trying to prove that he can work hard and pull well . . . Don't laugh. These oxen are very smart. The old one lets the young one do most of the work. But when the going gets tough, they work together like a team of magnificent chariot horses."

"So if you're an ox pulling under the yoke, how much burden you have to carry depends on who you're yoked with."

"Yes, see? Now you are thinking like an ox."

The weather was just as much a trial as any banditry or misfortune. Their northerly route brought the caravan closer each day to harsh conditions. While the nights had been cool since their departure, they were now getting down right cold. Campfires were started earlier each evening. People lingered around their fires as long as possible each morning. The pack animals and beasts of burden were harder to rouse and to load or yoke. The sheep and goats seemed not to mind, their fleece keeping the weather at bay.

Before Levi altered his course to a more northeasterly direction he halted the caravan for a lengthy rest and a time for trading. He had a number of sheep cut out of the flock and took carts filled with tools and leather away with him. Several horsemen accompanied him. Other outriders patrolled the length of the caravan keeping an eye on the horizon. The flocks were brought in closer for security.

Levi had been gone for a day when the outriders gave the alarm that there were horsemen and carts approaching. This stirred more excitement among the people of the caravan than it did alarm. The outriders were paid to be suspicious. Their share of the profits depended upon them keeping the caravan safe. However, those approaching wanted only an opportunity to trade with the caravan.

Dried food and spices were available. But the food items were not the first items to be traded. The experienced travelers of the caravan went directly to those merchants who were dealing in warm blankets and robes. There was some fur available for a very dear price. The weather would be turning very cold. Better to be prepared with as much warm clothing as was possible. Yeshua had not packed any heavy clothing. He now traded for a fine robe that could also serve as a blanket.

Only when most of the cloth was gone did the trading for food and spices begin in earnest. The merchants brought wine. This wine was lighter in color and thinner than the wine they had carried from home. Their wine skins had recently begun to empty so this was a good time to replenish both the wine and the wineskins.

That night great fires were built and fresh meat was cooked. The merchants danced and told stories. Some fanciful, some believable. The more believable stories concerned bandits and robbers known to be lurking in the foothills directly to the north. Winter seemed to be making an early appearance this year. The bandits were very bold in laying in their stores for the coming cold weather. However this was to be done at the expense of others. The stories told of bandits sneaking in under the cover of darkness and making off with the flock. Other stories told of brazen acts and murder as caravans were plundered. Our caravan, they said, was too large. We should not worry.

Yeshua noted that the merchants who brought young

women with them commanded a higher price for their
goods. They also traded a good deal more wine. They also
got a lot of attention from the men of the caravan. Yeshua
was reminded of the time in Greece when Yosuf had warned
him away. Trading should be honorable, not reduced to
trickery. However, he was satisfied that he had made a good
trade and otherwise enjoyed the stories. People always told
stories.

Levi had turned the caravan toward the east of north.
Perhaps he too had heard the tales of bandits to the north
and wanted to avoid them. Yeshua believed that Levi had intended this course change all along. After all, he and his father had lead many caravans. Whatever the reason for the
course change, the caravan was colder and more wary than
it had been since they left home.

Several days into this northeasterly trek a lone horse
was spotted standing against the horizon. The horse was
riderless. Levi wondered aloud why the horse wasn't running with a herd. Even more puzzling was the fact that it
did not bolt at the sight of the caravan. Levi concluded that
the animal had been tamed. Which meant that there were
men about, possibly hostile. Levi ordered the caravan to
halt. He posted guards all along the caravan and ordered
that the flocks be brought in closer. Wary now the caravan
took a defensive position as Levi and some of his most
trusted men rode off to investigate.

Levi's return was the occasion for much talk up and
down the line. All could see Levi leading the horse with two
individuals riding, one much smaller than the other, no big-

ger than a child. This is where I enter the story, you see, I was that child.

A crowd gathered around Levi as he led the horse with a woman and a boy atop back toward the caravan. Caravaners flocked around him. There was barely room for him to dismount. But the crowd parted to make room. Mostly out of respect, but still they wanted to hear the story.

Levi began, "It appears that a small band of traders was over taken by robbers. The men had been cut down by swordsmen; the women and children carried off. This woman as you can see was covered in blood when we found her. We took her for dead.

"The carts had been ransacked. But still we will take what we can find." He then ordered a party of men accompanied by outriders to scavenge the area where the attack had taken place. They were to salvage any of the carts that were sound and load them with any goods and food left behind.

Continuing the story, Levi said, "This woman was lying beside a man whose neck and shoulder had been sliced open. Blood was everywhere. We thought she had been killed, too. When we went to reclaim any weapons that we could find, she jumped up and attacked us. Fiercely defending the body, or so we thought. She must be a little crazy to fight for a dead body.

"But, no. She was defending her son. She had covered her son with her husband's dead body and then thrown herself down along side of them in order to conceal the boy. After the robbers had fled with their booty, she cautiously searched around for a weapon and some food for her and her son. She managed to coerce this lone horse back to camp by talking quietly and offering it some vegetables.

"When she saw us she feared that we were the robbers returning to claim that which had been left behind. She let the horse go free hoping we would chase it, but the horse just stood there. Once again she covered her son with her husband's dead body, smeared blood all over herself and then threw herself over the boy.

"When we approached to investigate, she jumped up to defend. We did not advance on her, but set to discovering what could be claimed from the aftermath. She soon realized that we meant her and the boy no harm. She was distraught. She began to tell us of the attack. The retelling seemed to calm her a little. When she regained some of her composure she offered herself as a slave to the caravan in return for protection for her son. I have accepted her offer.

"I claim the horse as mine." He then yelled, "Yeshua! This woman and this boy are yours! They will join your campfire. The boy will help with the flocks. Show them to your fire, then scour the area for scattered animals. Return before nightfall."

Yeshua tried not to show his perplexity. He was glad for the assigned task of reclaiming lost animals. He hastily led the woman and child to the cart that served as the center of activity for the herdsmen. As the cart was at the far end of the caravan Yeshua and the woman had plenty of time to talk. However, there was no talking. The woman knew her place. She would not speak unless spoken to. Yeshua was bombarded with new things to think about. And was not ready to say anything.

The woman knew her business. She set about organizing the camp and preparing the food. She needed no instruction.

Yeshua thankfully viewed his task of searching for stray animals as a time to get used to his new situation. Up to now he had been alone with his thoughts. He could meditate as he walked. He could ponder. He could wonder at the heavens. He could interact with the other herdsmen as he wished. Or be off by himself and be silent. By now he and his comrades had become accustomed to each other, could read moods. Mostly they left Yeshua to journey alone. But now, now this woman and this boy!

Levi smiled to himself as he watched Yeshua go out in search of the animals. Levi just shook his head as Yeshua set off in a direction most shepherds would not go. Yeshua would make a large circle route and then return to the caravan. Still he knew if there were animals to be found, Yeshua would find them. He worried that Yeshua would take his assignment too seriously and stay away longer than Levi wanted him to.

Indeed, he did not return before nightfall as ordered. He did return before sunrise though, reasoning that the caravan would not get started until morning any way. He found one lamb that had been too tired to keep up with the flock that had been run off. He also found two horses. He imagined that he must have been a sight to those in the caravan as he approached with a lamb across his shoulders, carrying his staff and leading two horses.

Over the next weeks the caravan set into a predictable rhythm. They would march for two or three days and then

rest a day. There appeared to be no one to trade with along
this stretch. Sometimes when the weather was particularly
cold Levi would push them into a fourth day of travel just to
keep them going.

One evening Yeshua asked my mother, "What is your
name?"

"Petranilla."

"A Roman name. You do not look to be Roman."

"I am not Roman. My mother was a slave to a Roman
family so she gave me a Roman name. I was given in marriage to Sander when I was a young girl. Sander was a powerful man. He is the one they found dead. He is the boy's
father. Sander took great pride in his son," my mother said
with a flair and a pride of her own. "He said his son would
inherit his wealth some day. Although Sander was not as
great as Levi, still he was a proud and noble man. He was
an honest trader."

"Ah, an honest trader."

The sleeping arrangements were a little complicated as
far as Yeshua was concerned. Before Petranilla came on the
scene he would simply roll himself in his robe and sleep as
close to the fire as he could. Rarely did he erect the leather
canopy for his own protection. Now the canopy was raised
every night and struck every morning. Petranilla tended the
fire and cooked the meals. He had to admit that the meals
had improved. She had a way with spices and stews that
made each meal something to look forward to.

Out with the flocks keeping warm was less of a prob-
lem. They would shelter the animals for the night as best
they could. The animals would usually generate enough

heat to warm them through the night. I always accompanied Yeshua, learning as we went. Petranilla stayed with the caravan.

When it was Yeshua's time to return to the caravan after tending the animals for so many days his comrades began to find his return most amusing.

"Yeshua, you will have some of that good food tonight, yes?" or "Yeshua, it looks to be a cold night but you will keep warm, eh?" Then laughter.

And so they settled into a routine. Yeshua seemed to enjoy instructing me. He found it a pleasant distraction I think.

Levi had been watching the horizon for several days now. His gaze was constant and his mood was impatient. The cold wind blowing down from the now visible mountains made everyone a little irritable. Levi was beyond irritable.

His mood abruptly changed as an outrider came racing back. There was a large caravan approaching, headed south.

"Who is in the lead?" more of a demand than a question from Levi.

"It is Amnon."

When the caravan masters finally met, Levi said, "Amnon, my old friend. I have been watching for you these many days."

"And I you, Levi. I see you are leading a very impressive caravan. Much wealth to be gained. I don't remember your father ever leading such a large caravan. He would be proud. Maybe he would have his eye on his share of the profits, eh?

Levi laughed with his friend at this apparent accurate caricature of his father. Levi knew that Amnon missed his father almost as much as Levi had. They were long time friends who found honest men in each other in a business not known for honest men.

"How many days can you spare?"

"I am not sure, Amnon, what is your advice?"

"The weather further north is cold but you can endure it. You will not encounter the great snows until you are higher up. If you are heading east, I think you will have little difficulty. We should stay two, three days. No longer than three I should think."

So it was settled. The caravans would camp together for two days and depart on the third, each going their own separate way.

I recall that each caravan began to set up its own encampment. They found themselves on a plain. Not the best of rest stops along the way. But the excitement and anticipation of interaction with these traders overcame the discomfort of the cold. Amnon encamped on the west side of the plain, Levi on the east. In the middle was the meeting ground. It was here that the great fires would burn into the night surrounded by story telling, trading and friendly banter.

Amnon's flocks were thinned out from the long travel. He needed to replenish his sheep and goats. Horses were needed. He didn't appear to need any oxen. He had camels. Camels were used as pack animals that would carry large loads. What Levi's people would load into carts, Amnon's people would load onto camels. Each caravan had its own system.

Amnon touted the advantages of the durability and worth of camels while Levi discounted them as stubborn and nasty, spitting beasts. Levi touted the advantages of ox carts as dependable and predictable while Amnon believed them to be something that was always in need of repair. Yeshua said to me that it was evident that the two had had this type of friendly banter before. Neither changing the other's mind.

Yeshua was mindful of the late nights, the singing and dancing, the story telling, the trading and the arguing. But these were not the events of that time that stood out in his mind. No, the events he recalled most vividly were about his slave, my mother, Petranilla.

The one incident about birthing a child happened on the first night of the encampment. Amnon was not particular about how many women accompanied the men of his caravan. Whether slaves or wives he was not concerned. Each woman was the concern of the man who brought her. Levi discouraged women from traveling with his caravan. He thought women were a distraction from the needs of the caravan and a source of friction among the men. So, on that night, the first incident concerning women occurred. Amnon came to Levi with a request.

"Levi, one of my families is in need. Can you help this man?"

Amnon, having made the request and the introductions, departed. "How can I be of assistance," Levi said with some curiosity in his voice. After all what could he provide that Amnon could not?

"My woman is about to give birth, I think her time has come. Our midwife died in the mountains some months ago. We have no one to assist with the birth, except for our shepherds who are used to assisting sheep with difficult births."

"I see. So you want a midwife?"

"Yes."

"That particular skill is not needed much in my caravans, but I will send someone to inquire. You can pay?"

"Yes, I can pay."

Levi sent an underling to gather the few women from the caravan and inquire if anyone had skill as a midwife. Petranilla was one such skilled. "I have assisted in the birth of many babies for my husband's people. I know what to do."

It was settled, Petranilla would be the one to go.

She returned to the cart more out of respect for Yeshua than for the need to collect belongings. She didn't have much in the way of belongings to collect but she did want to speak to Yeshua. She wanted to seek permission from her master to undertake this task. She knew that Yeshua would understand. He pretty much left her to her own devises anyway. This was a formality she understood better than Yeshua did.

"Master, a woman in Amnon's caravan is heavy with child. I have the skills to help her. If it is your wish, I will go and see what I can do."

"Is this the man's wife or the man's slave?"

"Wife, slave, it is all the same from the woman's point

of view." Petranilla knew from her association with Yeshua that he would not reprimand her for her insolent talk. She always spoke plainly. What difference did it make if it was a wife or a slave? Her time was near.

"Men!" she said half out of exasperation and half out of amusement. Yeshua nodded his assent. Petranilla headed off in the direction of Amnon's caravan.

The second incident was a direct result of the first. Petranilla's skills were more than suited for the task she undertook. Though a slave, she drew notice to herself through her skill and her bearing. The new mother and her baby boy were now doing well. The birth was not routine. How could a birth in the middle of the wilderness be routine? Petranilla had assisted at much more difficult births. But this was the first one with a camel as a backdrop.

Levi summoned Yeshua to his campfire on that second night. It seemed that Amnon's man who had lost his wife in the mountains lost more than a wife. He also lost the income she produced with her skills as a midwife and as a healer. The man now wanted to buy Petranilla for his wife. Levi had pretty much struck the bargain but left the final decision to Yeshua.

Yeshua listened as the man recounted his story and his need. All the while Yeshua maintained unwavering eye contact with the man, trying to discern the wholesomeness of his soul. What kind of husband would he be? How would he treat Petranilla? In the end Yeshua said nothing. Only nodded his head in assent.

He took the pouch of coins and returned to his own campfire. He crouched down on his haunches in front of the

Do.

fire next to Petranilla. Yeshua then placed the pouch of coins inside a fold in her robe. She started to speak but Yeshua quieted her with by bringing his fingers to his lips.

He then spoke gently to her. "You will be the wife of Amnon's man. He is a good man and an honest trader. Together you will enjoy a long life. You will bear him children and help him prosper. In your old age your children and grandchildren will be a blessing to you. The money I have given you is the price I received for you. This is the only secret that you are to keep from your new husband that you have this money. You will know when you must use it."

Petranilla absorbed all he said through tearless eyes. She knew she had sealed her fate when she offered herself up to Levi as a slave. She silently gathered her things including the spices she had accumulated. The wife of a caravan trader must know how to cook. Yeshua made no objection to this even though all that she took was, under the law, really his.

"You will come to me again, won't you, Master? So that I can serve you again?" my mother said with quiet dignity and a certainty I did not understand.

With comforting assurance, "Yes," was all he replied.

Saying nothing more, Petranilla walked toward Levi's campfire with her head held high. A bearing that Yeshua knew that he would miss. I thought I was to go with my mother so I followed along with her.

"Son of Sander," Yeshua called. "You will stay with me. We will be off to the sheep and goats this night. Gather some food. I will be back shortly."

I looked at my mother. When she nodded her assent, I

turned back to do what I was told. The sadness and empti-
ness that I felt was masked by the task that I must do.
Yeshua was understanding. Over the next days and weeks
he was both a comfort and a teacher and a father. I miss her
still, but that is another story.

I learned later from Levi that Yeshua returned to Levi's
campfire after my mother had departed with her new
husband.

"Levi, here is your share of the sale of Petranilla."
Yeshua saying this hoping he was not revealing too much of
his emotion to Levi.

"Yes, I knew you would return with my share, Yeshua.
That is why I did not ask you for it in front of the others.
You are an honest trader. But I have been thinking. You gave
your share to Petranilla didn't you? Now don't say anything,
I know that is what you would do. Keep my share for the
boy. Can I allow you to be more generous than I am? Cer-
tainly not."

"The boy earns his own way," was all Yeshua could
think to say.

"Yes, I know the boy is a good worker. Still you or he
may have need of it some day. Keep it."

As Yeshua and I were returning to the flocks, Yeshua
could only ponder the fact that other people seemed to
know him better than he knew himself. To me he said little.
Yeshua was lost in his own thoughts and he left me to mine.

*Ah, Phillip, that must have been a sad time for you. To be
separated from your mother.*

It was at first, as you might imagine, but the adventures for a young boy were plentiful. And the real adventure was about to begin.

"I will look for you in ten months time," Yeshua said to Levi.

"Ten months, a year, that is about right," said Levi.

Yeshua and I turned to the northwest; Levi and the caravan went east. It was his purpose to leave the caravan, you see. He was being called away. Though he didn't tell me this at the time, I just sensed it.

It was Yeshua's intent all along to journey alone for a while and abide in a city he had heard of. I would be a concern for him that he had not considered, but he had traveled with his father as a young boy so there was no reason why he and I could not go on together. It was settled.

The caravan would not be stopping to trade with merchants of this city. It was too far off and Levi did not want to take chances with the coming of the colder weather. So Yeshua and I made our own way.

The city gate was closed when Yeshua and I reached it. We spent the night with several traders and travelers who were forced to wait through the night for morning when the city gates would be opened. The campfires were communal though each party kept their food to themselves. The night passed peacefully enough. It was the morning when trouble began to brew.

Sunlight had roused most of the people outside this particular gate. The clank and bustle of people gathering their things together and otherwise breaking camp roused the remainder. The gate would soon be opened.

Yeshua and I joined the others on the road leading up to the city in anticipation of the opening of the gate. Conversations were in evidence up and down the road as the traders gathered their burdens and travelers brushed the dust off their clothes. Yeshua was engaged in just such a conversation with a traveler who had been to this city before. Yeshua, his back to the road, was inquiring about the layout of the city and where he might find certain places. The man he was talking to kept trying to edge Yeshua further and further off the road.

The warning look came too late as Yeshua felt intense pain across the back of his neck and his shoulder. He had apparently been struck from behind, the blow knocking him to the ground. Ignoring the pain Yeshua jumped back up and with nostrils flaring turned to face his attacker. He was struck again, this time in the face with the handle of a whip. He once again fell to the ground.

"Get out of my way vagabond!" the man shouting at Yeshua. "I am of noble birth and have the right of way. You must get off the road when I pass by with my goods. Has no one taught you? You could be severely punished for failing to offer due respect. This little beating should teach you a valuable lesson."

Yeshua endured this tirade from the ground propped up on one elbow. He took in the man and how he was dressed, his carts, and the servants who accompanied him. The servants did not make eye contact with their master and would not make eye contact with Yeshua. Conversations up and down the road ceased. All eyes now focused on the shouting nobleman. Those close by backing away.

Yeshua stood, very slowly. He faced his attacker and then walked by him to the first cart. Yeshua perched one bundle on his left shoulder and lifted the other bundle under his right arm. Bending with the load, he carried the man's goods up to the gate and set them down. He then returned to the one manservant who seemed to have the heaviest burden, removed the burden from him and that too he carried to the gate.

The nobleman was confused and perplexed into silence. But he had enough presence to follow Yeshua up the road the second time. As Yeshua turned from the pile of goods he had delivered to the gate he found himself once again face to face with his attacker.

"You are a very powerful man. You have carried not one but two burdens uphill and uttered not one word of protest. You have the bearing of one who walks with authority, yet you did not challenge me or fight back. Why?"

"If I had struck you in retaliation, then I would be like you. It is better if you would be like me."

The man raised his whip handle to strike yet another blow across Yeshua's face for he could not be expected to endure such an insult in front of so many people who had seen and heard all. Yeshua did not move. Only looked into the man's eyes.

The nobleman slowly lowered his arm. As he lowered his arm a slight smile began to cross his face. As he smiled more so did Yeshua smile. Soon the man was laughing and moving away from Yeshua. He gestured to his servants to gather up his goods as the gate was being raised. He assumed his rightful place at the head of the procession to be allowed entry into the city. The nobleman said no more neither did he look back.

Those who bore witness to this event began to assemble toward the gate. Some wore astonished looks. Some just looked at Yeshua and shook their heads; others just passed by not understanding any of what they just had seen.

There were no more incidents such as this. We looked around the city for several days. It was a large city with strange customs and different smells. We saw people who looked like Yeshua and worshiped with them. I was allowed to worship because I was with Yeshua. I got the feeling, though, that I would not have been admitted otherwise. Finally we came to a house that interested Yeshua. Our inquiries were answered by someone Yeshua seemed to know.

"Welcome. You have managed to gain some notoriety in the short time you have been here."

"It has taken me a few days to find you. I had to determine if I had the right place."

"You have the right place. I am sure."

"What then of this notoriety?"

"Come in, we will get you and the boy situated and fed. Then I will tell you anything you wish to know. But of your notoriety, surely you have seen the people in the market place and in the streets casting side glances at you as you went about your business?"

"I have noticed some such glances."

"The nobleman who beat you at the eastern gate to the city is famous for taking liberties with his position and station in life. He needs very little provocation to lash out with his tongue or his whip. Few dare to stand up to him. Even those higher in rank are intimidated by his outbursts. Yet you calmed him. People talk. It was then that I knew who you were and that you would find your way here."

Yeshua and I were settled. After sleeping out in the open for so many months and then having such shabby accommodations in the city I had a hard time falling asleep amid such splendor. I gazed at the wall hangings taking in the elegance of the tapestry and the stories they told. The floor seemed to glow in the firelight. I had heard of pillows, sure, but this is the first time I ever got to sleep on one. I had a full belly and a weary body but at long last I fell asleep. Yeshua and the sage, however, talked into the night.

Later, he told me of their conversations. Some I did not understand then. After visiting with Yeshua's family and learning the recent events, I have a new understanding and appreciation of what he told me and the journey he had to make.

"You came to visit me," said Yeshua.

"Yes," replied the sage.

"How did you know where to go?" he wanted to know.

"An old man sitting in the shade of a tree directed us."

"Was he singing?"

"Yes."

"I know this old man!" After a long silent pause of reflection Yeshua continued quietly, "You know, my mother never sold those things you brought although I suspect the perfume has long since evaporated. She never would permit my father to use the gold, even in the harshest of times. She still has it."

"Yes, I believe that is so. . . . You had a very interesting king back then. He was a devious and suspicious sort of fellow. I don't think he liked you. Though what there is about a child not to like I do not know."

"I have heard stories of such a king. We left for a while and lived in another place while my father worked as a laborer and traded when he could. That is where I met the old man. He was a great teacher and fun to be with. There were no children around. The old man was good company."

At this point in the conversation they were interrupted by a servant wishing to know if more pillows were needed or if the two desired more tea. Their comfort assured, the conversation continued.

Yeshua asked, "What of the others who visited me? I would speak with them also."

"They no longer live in this world."

"I understand. Still, it would have been nice to meet them."

Other conversations throughout the next weeks and months were not as profound. Others were profound beyond meaning. Yeshua talked about the caravan and the people he met along the way. He talked of growing up. He talked of the circumstances surrounding why I was with him. He shared his long time association with Levi. Learning the scriptures from the old man was a theme Yeshua returned to often. He was in awe of the way the old man could sing the old stories from his heart, never needing as much as a glance at the written scrolls that other rabbis used.

After we had been there for a time the others tired of calling me "Son of Sander." I was often in the company of other young men who were sent there to study. They are the ones who gave me the name "Phillip." I quickly learned the nuance of languages foreign to my own tongue. I was quite taken with the concept of mathematics as known in this land. Mathematics was something that even the great Sander, my father, did not know, though he could calculate profit well enough. So I concentrated on mathematics.

I was off with other scholars under the tutelage of clerics. Yeshua and the sage were left with plenty of time to spend in each other's company. Indeed, the sage had passed off his teaching duties to others so he could spend time with Yeshua exclusively.

Yeshua remembered long and complicated discussions that lasted into the night. Often the two would be so engaged in conversation that they were heedless of sleep or the need to eat. Other days would pass in total silence. Their meditation uninterrupted by even the most doting of servants.

Yeshua shared the experience of Petranilla. "You know when Levi gave Petranilla to me the other herdsmen found it quite comical. They joked about keeping warm on cold nights. They laughed when I tried to teach the boy about our animals. They said, 'He is not your son. Why do you bother with such as he?' And when we were at camp they would make fun of our food saying that it probably was not as good as what I was eating when Petranilla cooked. And then when she was sold off in marriage they continued to tease but now it was because they thought I was missing all that and comment must be made in the most lewd manner. . . . I understand the humor, learned sage, but I do not always comprehend the world of men."

"You have told me that you have experienced the world of men and that the world of men is harsh. But have you considered why their world is so harsh? The world of men is so harsh because they can find no meaning in life deeper than their own flesh. . . . You have been reflecting on this your whole life. You must teach them to be otherwise."

"But, what must I teach?"

"What lesson did you learn from the nobleman who beat you?"

"I did not want him to strike me so I did not strike him."

"Ah, just so," said the sage. Do not do unto others what you do not want others to do unto you."

"There seems like there should be more than that."

"There is. You must teach them to do as you do. Look into the depths of your soul for the meaning of life. Don't you see, Yeshua, that you must be a prophet? Lead your people to your God."

Yeshua did not answer for a long time. There was an awkward silence between them. Yeshua said finally and in a very small voice, "We kill our prophets."

"Then you must be more than a prophet—be a leader. Lead your people to your God."

Yeshua tried to lead the sage away from this type of discussion. "Do you lead people to your god?" Yeshua remembered he tried to throw the sage off, not willing to grasp what should be, what must be grasped.

"Yes."

"But your god does not have the same name as Yahweh."

The sage showing a great deal of patience now, "Who can name the one true God? We humans give a name to our gods in a vain attempt to capture them for our own purposes. The one true God has no human name. We are just comforted to think that He does."

The sage now skillfully drawing Yeshua back into the original conversation, "You have shared with me all these months that you have been conscious of a watchful Presence your whole life. The Presence has been with you so long that you now feel that you are one with the Presence and the Presence is one with you. You must teach men that this Presence can be with them also. You are the way to truth. You are the way to life. Why do you think we came to you all of those years ago? To find the way."

"I am the way?" a barely audible whisper from Yeshua.

"Yes, you are the way," a quietly reaffirming statement from the sage.

"I am the way," this time with recognition and acceptance.

The sage moved slowly, noiselessly away. Yeshua was left alone in the Presence.

He considered things like food. The purpose of food was to feed the flesh and keep it alive. But what keeps the soul alive? It is the soul that must be nourished if man is to be truly kept alive. The breath of God must enter the soul. The breath of God is food for the soul. As a cool wind comforts the laborer as well as the nobleman so too does the breath of God comfort the soul of all who would receive it. And so he thought. And so he grew with the Spirit.

Aren't people like sheep? He considered. When sheep

stay together doing what sheep do there is no trouble. You protect the sheep from danger. When one wanders off you go fetch it and bring it back. But bring it back to what?

He addressed this question to the sage. "What must I bring men back to?"

The sage in his wisdom knew that Yeshua already knew the answer. The sage only helped him to find it. He asked, "What is the purpose of men? What did your ancient leaders do?"

"The purpose of man is to worship Yahweh, to honor the Creation. . . . Our leaders and our prophets brought man back to God."

"You must bring men back to God." Once again the sage departed to leave Yeshua alone with his thoughts and his God.

Rest a moment, Phillip, while I tell you this. Yeshua did not talk to us of sheep. Those stories he told to others. He talked to us of fish. But it is the same thing. I always thought that one day he was just filled with the Spirit and began his ministry like so many others. But he is not like the others. He has taken his whole life to learn. His journey has led him to us. Maybe even beyond us.

And so it is, Mark. But let me tell you the rest so that you will know the full measure of his heart.

Ever since his experience with the healer on that second journey, the one where he went with his father, he has been pondering the fate of the sick and the afflicted. Why, he wondered out loud, were there so many who were not well?

Why would God permit such a thing? And why would the priests of your temple push those who were ill away from God rather than embrace them?

Yes, yes. He was always catering to the infirm, the unwashed, and the unwanted.

And so you begin to understand what Yeshua already understood. Are not the infirm, the unwashed and the unwanted also part of Creation? Are they not entitled to worship God? Are they not entitled to our compassion? It is not for us to know why we have been given gifts to use or diseases to endure; that appears to be the business of life, God's business. But Yeshua made it his business to reach out to the afflicted and bring them into the fold of the Creator's love.

All this he thought about. All of this he pondered. And he grew in the Spirit.

The next few months passed by seemingly in one beat of the heart. Yeshua saw the sage and me almost daily. Sometimes he and the sage and I would share a meal. But most of his time was now spent in quiet meditation. My progress as a young scholar, I am pleased to tell you, was accelerating. I learned fast because that is what Yeshua wanted me to do. In the meantime, Yeshua and the sage had reached that point where the sage could no longer be his spiritual guide. The sage withdrew. Yeshua was left to his own meditations. He became his own spiritual guide. As he meditated he grew stronger. Even when he forgot to eat, he grew stronger in his meditations.

"I am the Way," he would tell himself. He would focus his thoughts around, "I am the Way."

Oh, Phillip, so often he said to us, "I am the Way." But thanks to your story we have reached new understanding. We did not always understand what he was saying. It seems he was speaking to the multitudes about one thing and urging us to consider some other, even more meaningful, message.

Let me continue, Mark.

Then one day it was my pleasure to greet Yeshua with the news that a caravan was approaching the city. Though it was still a few days off, rumor was that it was Levi's caravan.

The preparations for departure were few. Yeshua had always known this day would come. That he would return to his homeland to fulfill all that had to be fulfilled. I was not happy to be left behind. I still held onto a boy's sense of adventure. If you must know the truth, I had forgotten the hard work and deprivation that accompanied such a long march. I only remembered that it was out in the open air that I was happiest. That was where, once in time, my father, my mother and I had been a family. It was where I walked and learned with my Yeshua. It was where I wanted to be.

Yeshua sat me down for a quiet talk. "In the last year you have lost your father to murderous bandits. Your mother was given in marriage to another man. And now I am leaving you here and traveling on alone. You have suffered loss. But you can abide here and study and learn. Here among the sage, the clerics and the scholars you will have a family. New adventures await you. You must be patient."

Turning to the sage Yeshua asked, "You will send him to me?"

"Yes, I will send him."

Yet again addressing me he said, "You will be sent to me when I need you. In the mean time you must stay here and learn the languages. You may dabble in your mathematics as you wish, but you must learn the languages in earnest."

Yeshua silently handed over the pouch of money from Levi's share of the sale of Petranilla. The sage took the money with a nod. The unspoken understanding was that the money would be used for my schooling and future travel.

The reunion with Levi was joyous. New faces were evident in the caravan. Stories of old friends who had settled out along the way or who had decided to remain in the east were shared. The caravan continued to be profitable. An expectant air was about the caravan. Profits had been made; profits would continue to be made until they reached home. Levi was a great caravan master.

"Yeshua, I am in need of someone who can keep the carts in good repair. I could also use your good eyes and your strong arm as an outrider. But let me guess, you want your old job back. Always the shepherd. Am I right?"

"Yes, Levi, I will be numbered among your herdsmen."

I returned to the city. Yeshua left with the caravan quickly falling into old, familiar travel. But now the travel was toward home. I watched him go. I did not cry, though I wanted to. I knew that I would rejoin him.

You will rejoin him my friend; but perhaps not as you originally thought.

I learned from Miriam that the caravan home went quickly as one day blurred into another either stopping time for Yeshua or speeding it up. He could not decide which. He avoided the inevitable dust as often as he could. The caravan and the herds that followed kicked up enormous amounts of dry, choking dust. When he could not lead the flocks of sheep off to one side on a parallel path with the caravan Yeshua simply endured.

He did not rejoin the caravan as the herdsmen often did. He would give up his turn to enjoy a hot cooked meal and the warmth of a large campfire to a fellow herdsman choosing instead to stay out under the sun and the stars with only Yahweh as his companion.

A plan was formulating in his mind. But he needed more time to think about it, to refine it. He knew about man and he knew about God. How could he reconcile the two? He must do it? That was his purpose. He knew that now for a certainty.

His family was, of course, overjoyed to see him. However, his return home was met with some sadness. Yosuf had died. A wall of stone had fallen on his father and crushed him. Many bones were broken. He lingered only a short while and then he died. Yeshua grieved.

It is true he did not suffer well the loss of those close to him.

I am sure that that is true, Mark.

His brothers were now supporting their mother and the one sister who had not yet married. A day or so had passed when Yeshua finally found himself alone with Miriam. He recounted for his mother all that had passed in the years he was gone. He needed for her to know all that he reflected upon. He gave her his share of the profit from his work with the caravan. She said she did not need it. In that case, he said that she should keep the money safe. She would know when it was time to be spent.

As his mother learned more and more of what he intended she became increasingly agitated. "I have lost a husband. Must I now lose a son? They will surely kill you."

"You will not lose me, you will never lose me," he said to her.

She could not be reassured. Pleading for an alternative she said, "Instead of this why don't you take time to write down all you have seen and all you have done? People can learn from you."

"It will be for others to write."

After a long time of quiet her tone had changed. Resignedly she asked, "Then what happens now?"

"Now it begins."

"Now it begins?" That is what he said? "Now it begins?" Don't you see that that is what we should do. Now it begins for us too. This is what we must do. We will send to Peter. He will know how we should be organized. If our Yeshua is the

way as He said He was, then we must show others the way through His example. Others must become aware of their own spiritual journey. They must open their hearts and care for their souls and the soul of mankind as Yeshua did. Now it begins for us. Now it begins for them. Now it begins for everyone. We all journey in the spirit don't we? We must tell the story. Phillip, you must write down all that you know. Those who do not hear the story from us must read about it for this is truly a journey we all must take. It is now up to us to tell the story.

Mark, you may begin by telling me all that has occurred since Yeshua and I parted. If I am to write, I need to hear about the latter days of his journey. After being here by your side I have come to believe that Yeshua's journey is a journey without end. Indeed, now it begins.

Look for the *Now It Begins Spiritual Guide Handbook* due for publication later this year. This is an easy-to-read guide that will help you answer questions you may have about your own spiritual journey. It is written in simple language and is designed to be a starting point. The *Now It Begins Spiritual Guide Handbook* offers easy to follow suggestions and provides further resources for the seeker.

As a retired educator, I have taken what I have learned from over thirty years in education and combined that with the experiences of my own spiritual journey. Part of my mission is to assist or guide people on their spiritual journeys. If you desire further information about your spiritual journey, please contact me at yellow.finch@sbcglobal.net.

I am available for talks, seminars, discussion groups, and book clubs. For further information contact me at Yellow Finch.

Cliff Mulvihill